The P
A Wing and a Prayer Mystery
featuring Gertrude, Gumshoe

ROBIN MERRILL

New Creation Publishing
Madison, Maine

Dedicated to the amazing Miss Jodi, the
best of the best!
We are so grateful for you!

Chapter 1

Nate gave his wife a long kiss. Then he flashed her a sweet smile.

Sandra couldn't help being suspicious. "What do you want?"

He laughed, and the genuineness of it warmed her heart. "I don't want anything. Can't I kiss my wife for no reason? Actually, that's not true. I do want something. How about we call Ethel and get her to come babysit tonight? I'll take you out to a fancy dinner."

"I'm too old for a babysitter," Peter called from the living room. "Also, *gross!*"

They both laughed at their eldest son.

"I think we should kiss in front of him more often," she said softly.

"Gross!" Peter called again.

Sandra patted her husband on the chest. "I would *love* to go out to dinner." They hadn't been to a sit-down restaurant in months. And a sit-down restaurant without their children along? Years. "But I can't tonight. Joanna has her first dance class."

He frowned and stepped back. "Dance class?"

She didn't understand his confusion. Joanna had been jabbering about it for weeks.

"Dance class. From four to six. She's so excited."

"But I thought we decided we weren't going to do that. Because she's too young." He pulled a wooden chair away from their kitchen table and sat. "I've seen videos of young girls in recitals, and they don't even dance. They barely stay in their line. They come out on stage and then squint in the lights and look for their parents."

She narrowed her eyes, pretending to study him. "Why are you watching recital videos of little girls?"

He laughed. "I'm not, on purpose, but everyone posts them on social media. You know. Anyway, I don't want to pay someone for a whole year when she's too little to even dance."

"She's not too little." She tried to keep her voice even. She didn't want this to turn into an argument. "She dances all the time." This was true. She danced during church music, in her booster seat to minivan music, and during any television commercial that had music. Sometimes she danced when there was no music.

"Exactly," he said.

Wait, what? What had she gotten right?

"She already dances enough. We don't need to pay for a year of it. We'll wait until she's older, and then if she's still interested, we can talk about it. Besides, another thing about those social media recitals? Those little girls aren't wearing enough clothes, and they're doing moves that aren't appropriate for anyone, let alone little girls."

Sandra shook her head vehemently. "I did my research, Nate. I would never let Joanna participate in something that wasn't good for her. This is a classy school, the best in the area. It's run by an accomplished dancer, teacher, and choreographer named Joyelle—"

He snorted. "*Joyelle.*"

"Yes, *Joyelle.* I think it's a lovely name. Anyway, she's got a resume three pages long. She's won a gazillion awards, and her school has competitive dance teams that win at everything."

He raised an eyebrow. "*Everything?*"

She had no idea. She didn't know how dance competitions worked. She took a deep breath. "Nate, I already told her she could do this—"

"Why did you tell her that when I said she couldn't?"

"You never said that!" She was certain of this. She remembered the conversation. He hadn't seemed excited, but he hadn't forbidden it. He'd never looked up from his phone.

He scowled. He was getting angry.

"Nate, she is *so* excited. And I'll use my refereeing money to pay for it. It's not *that* expensive—"

"You say that now because you haven't paid for any costumes."

Now she was getting angry. She tried to control it, or at least hide it. "Like I said, when the time comes, I will be the one to pay for those." Thank heavens for soccer.

He clenched his jaw.

"And I already paid the deposit."

He let out a long breath. "Fine. But I'm not happy about it."

Yes, I gathered that already, she thought. She went to him, bent over, and kissed him lightly on the lips. "Thank you." She straightened. "We drive Peter all over tarnation for his activities, and Sammy takes up so much of my time and energy. I want to do something special for Joanna. She is my only little girl. She should get to do a little girl thing."

He arched an eyebrow. "Are you saying boys can't boogie?" He stood up and shook his hips back and forth in a terrifying attempt at dancing.

"Oh my word, Dad!" Peter called. "Please, make it stop!"

Sandra laughed, more at Peter's outburst than at Nate's attempt at rhythm. "I am not saying that, but you should stop before you hurt yourself." She squeezed his hand and went to the sink to finish the dishes. "Thank you. Wait until you see how happy it will make her. Then you'll be on board."

Chapter 2

Sandra needed coffee. "I'm going to swing through the Aroma Joe's drive-through," she said to the rearview mirror. "But I'm only getting some go-juice. No treats." It was tricky business taking a kid through a drive-through and not getting them anything, but she could usually pull it off.

Joanna ignored her. She was staring down at her tablet.

Sandra pulled her minivan into the long line and sighed. Why did this many people need coffee in the late afternoon? She looked in the mirror again. "Are you excited?"

Joanna didn't answer.

"Joanna?"

"What?" Oblivious.

"Honey, put the tablet away."

She groaned and turned it off.

"You don't need a tablet for a ten-minute car ride."

Joanna looked out the window and realized where they were. "Hey! Can I get a donut?"

Sandra shook her head and eased the car ahead. "No. We're not getting treats. Only coffee."

"But coffee *is* a treat for you."

This was not true. Coffee was a staple. "I said no."

She started to pout.

"I asked you if you were excited about your first dance class."

She nodded, looking out her window instead of looking at Sandra.

They waited in silence, easing the car ahead ten feet at a time. They were almost to the front of the line when Joanna announced that she had to go to the bathroom.

Sandra looked longingly at the squawk box and then met her daughter's eyes in the rearview. "Can you hold it for a few minutes? We'll be at the dance studio soon."

Joanna hesitated, but she had a pained look on her face.

"You've got to go pretty bad, huh?"

She nodded quickly.

"All right. Hang on." She pulled her van out of the line, and the car behind her filled the gap so fast it was as if she'd never been there. She found a parking spot, and then together they walked into Aroma Joe's, where the aroma was so fantastic it almost made the inside visit worthwhile. "Go ahead. I'm going to order."

Joanna scampered off, and Sandra got into a line that was a lot shorter than the one outside.

Like a tornado, a blond woman in Easter-egg-purple leggings burst through the door and headed toward the pickup arrow. She carried a large iced coffee in one hand and a giant collection of shiny key chains in the other. She had far more key chains than keys.

The young woman behind the counter turned to face her, and her expression spoke volumes. She reared back as she said, "Can I help—"

"I ordered soy milk!" the woman shrieked and slammed the cup down on the counter. Predictably, it cracked, and cold coffee started to leak out all over the counter.

Sandra's mouth watered at the sight of it.

"I'm sorry," the employee said. "I can make you another one?"

"Oh really?" the woman cried. "Can you also make it so I'm not late? Because you've made me late."

The young woman who had been managing the register left it to help her partner deal with the tempest. "We'd also like to give you a gift certificate, in addition to replacing your coffee today. What was your order again?"

The woman stepped back away from her cup, which continued to leak everywhere, folded her arms across her chest, and said, snottily, "Iced brown sugar cinnamon decaf with *soy milk*."

The cashier looked at her partner. "Go ahead and make it. I'll get the gift certificate."

Joanna came out of the bathroom and stopped, sensing the tension in the room. She looked around wide-eyed, and Sandra silently motioned to her to come stand with her in line. As she did this, the tornado snapped, "What are you looking at?" to the two people in front of Sandra in line.

Joanna slid her hand into Sandra's and then stared at the angry blonde.

The cashier handed the woman a gift card, gave her a forced smile, and said, "Thank you for your business."

The tornado took the card, looked down at it, and then shrieked, "Ten dollars? Are you kidding me? You said a gift card, not a coupon!" She threw the card back across the counter, but it traveled at a lazy speed that seemed to mock her anger, so she then picked up her faulty iced coffee and chucked it at the back of the young woman who was making her new coffee.

The poor girl let out a little shriek and arched her back at the shock of it. Sandra was glad then that half the drink had already leaked out onto the counter and was now dripping onto the floor.

"All right!" The man in the front of the line had decided to get involved, but it was too late. The tornado was already storming out the door. She had decided she didn't need her soy milk coffee after all.

The recipient of the ice bath was crying. The cashier wrapped her arms around her.

Sandra grabbed some napkins from the dispenser and went to tend to the counter flood. When that was cleaned up, they still hadn't completed the order of the first man in line, so Sandra grabbed Joanna's hand. "Come on, honey. I don't want you to be late for your first class."

Chapter 3

Synergy Dance Studio was abuzz with activity. They were having a bit of a kickoff party. A long table held a variety of festive snacks and a giant punch bowl. A television in the corner played a highlight reel of dance competitions gone by. Interspersed among clips of what Sandra thought to be professional-level dance moves were snippets of Synergy dancers accepting trophies. "I'd like to thank Miss Joyelle," a girl of about twelve said. "She's the best dance teacher in the world!" Some more flips and leaps and spins went by, and then a beautiful adult dancer with jewels stuck to her face held up a giant trophy for the camera. "I'd like to dedicate this to my mother. I miss you, Mom!"

Joanna tugged on Sandra's sleeve. "Can I have a brownie?"

"Sure."

Not wanting to travel across the room alone, her daughter pulled her over to the snack table. Now Sandra could smell the brownies. This was not a good thing. She tried not to look at them and scanned the room instead.

There were *so many* dancers. And they seemed so excited to see each other after their summer off. Parents looked stressed out, but also seemed to know one another, making Sandra feel a little left out. Joyelle appeared in the lobby.

"Miss Joyelle! Miss Joyelle!" the girls called out, chasing her around the room. Some of them had questions, and some wanted to tell her about their summer adventures, but most simply wanted her attention. Most simply wanted a hug from their dance teacher.

Sandra was confident they'd made the right decision. This was going to be good for Joanna. She smiled at her daughter, who looked nervous. "This is going to be so much fun!"

Joanna gave her a small smile and nodded. Then she shoved the rest of the brownie into her mouth. That hadn't lasted long.

Joyelle clapped her hands together. "Let's go into the studio, girls!" Despite Nate's protests, Sandra didn't see a single male student. All the girls followed Joyelle into the larger adjacent room.

Sandra tried to let go of Joanna's hand, but she tightened her grip. "It's okay, honey. I'll be right out here, and you're going to do great. Don't be nervous."

Joanna let go and scowled up at her mother. "I'm not nervous." Then slowly, she followed the rest of the class into the studio.

Parents were already clustered around the large viewing window, so Sandra found a seat and used her phone to check her reffing schedule. She would need to block all Tuesdays for the rest of the season because she would be spending those afternoons at Synergy, not on the soccer field.

A while later, Sandra looked at the clock, expecting that a good chunk of the class time had passed. It had not. She realized then that two hours a week in this room was going to be a bit of a sacrifice—especially when she'd have to bring Sammy along. Nate wouldn't always be available, or willing, to watch his son. She couldn't imagine how she was going to keep Sammy quiet in this room for two hours.

Her eyes scanned the room. The walls were lined with shelves, which were loaded with trophies. Synergy had been to a lot of competitions, and they had won a lot of trophies. Her eyes landed on a bulletin board where a poster announced the tryout dates for the various dance teams.

A flyer beside the poster caught her eye. A mother-daughter special. She squinted, trying to read the small print. A mother could take the adult class for free if her daughter was enrolled. She snickered. She couldn't imagine dancing. She'd made fun of her husband when he'd tried, but she didn't think she could do much better. But the next line tempted her. *If both mother and daughter were students, they would get a special duet in the recital.*

Sandra didn't want to be in the recital, but what a memory that would make! Talk about mother-daughter bonding. Joanna would remember that for the rest of her life. And they could have video and pictures … the thought of having to watch herself attempt to dance erased the temptation. It was a good deal and a lovely idea, but Sandra wasn't a dancer. She put the thought out of her mind and opened the Minecraft app on her phone. Then she joined a game of Egg Wars. She normally only played this with Peter and Joanna, but she could use the practice. She was fairly terrible at the game and usually relied on Peter to rescue her from precarious predicaments she found herself in. And now, playing without him, she had no one to rescue her, and she kept dying. At one point, when an opponent shot her off a bridge, she physically jumped in her chair, causing a few parents to eye her suspiciously. She gave them a peaceful smile that she hoped indicated she wasn't a lunatic and then went back to her game.

Of course, before long her phone chirped a low battery warning. She dug through her purse to find her charger and then located an outlet and borrowed some of Joyelle's electricity. A spot had opened up at the viewing window, and Sandra squeezed in. There was her little Joanna, right up front, pointing her toe out in front of her and tapping her foot on the floor. The move was as simple as simple could be and yet the beauty of it made her breath catch. Joanna's eyes studied Joyelle, who stood in front of her facing the mirror. Sandra couldn't remember ever seeing Joanna concentrate like that. Her little girl was growing up, was turning into a young woman right before her teary eyes.

Chapter 4

"Joanna was awesome!" Joyelle declared. "What a great first class! She is a born dancer."

"Thank you," Sandra managed, feeling shy all of a sudden. Joyelle's personality was so big and dazzling, it left Sandra a little star-struck.

"Are you a dancer?" Her smile was wide and charismatic.

"Who me? Uh … no."

"Never?"

Sandra shook her head.

"I find that hard to believe. She's such a natural. I figured it was in her genes."

An image of Joanna's father trying to "boogie" in the kitchen flashed through Sandra's mind, and she bit back a smile. If it was in Joanna's genes, then maybe her mother *could* dance after all.

"Do you know about our mother daughter special?" Joyelle asked.

Sandra nodded quickly. "Yes, that sounds like a great offer, but I don't think it's for me." She forced a smile. "Two left feet, you know." Her cheeks got hot. Why was she acting like such a dork? She had no idea.

Joyelle laughed, and it sounded like music. "You wouldn't be the first student to enter my studio lacking in confidence." She gave Sandra's arm an affectionate squeeze. "But I assure you, you are a fantastic dancer. You just don't know it yet. Let me know if you change your mind." She smiled down at Joanna. "Great job today, sweetie. Can't wait to see you next week!"

Joanna smiled. "Thank you," she said shyly.

The small lobby was filling up with women, and suddenly Sandra felt a little claustrophobic. She grabbed her purse, took Joanna's small hand, and gently tugged her toward the door. This wasn't easy, given the horde of women stretching their legs, changing their shoes, and chitchatting. And what a variety of women they were! All shapes, sizes, and styles.

There was the beautiful woman she'd seen on the video, though her face was no longer bejeweled. She looked a bit like a Barbie doll, but her sincere smile made her seem warm and real and not plastic.

Then there was a thoroughly tattooed woman with spiked black hair chatting with a very pregnant woman dressed in what looked like burlap. She was eagerly drinking green juice out of a mason jar. Sandra was certain that the juice didn't taste good, but the woman made it seem otherwise.

A woman wearing harem pants and a bindi was doing impressive stretches that took up a lot of room, visibly irritating an angry woman in a pantsuit, who was taking her frustration out on someone over a Bluetooth earpiece. Sandra wondered if she was a lawyer and then felt guilty for judging her. And judging lawyers.

Trying to avoid the pantsuit woman, Sandra pushed through the diverse crowd and was glad to reach the sidewalk, where she stopped to dig through her purse for her keys.

Once she'd found them, she unlocked the van and opened her door, which wasn't easy as someone had tucked a motorcycle between her vehicle and the one beside her. She assumed the bike belonged to the tattooed, spike-haired woman, but then silently scolded herself for such an assumption. It could just as easily belong to the pregnant woman. She almost laughed at the image as she closed the van's door behind her.

"Look!" Joanna cried, pointing through the windshield.

Sandra looked, and there she was: the tornado. Still wearing the Easter-egg-purple leggings. She now carried a giant bling-bling purse over one shoulder. And in her other hand, she held a large, half-full plastic cup from Starbucks. Sandra deduced that the beverage featured soy milk. The woman ripped open the dance studio door and nearly smashed into the tattooed woman.

"You're late," the tattooed woman said.

The tornado swore. "It's not like you can start without me."

The tattooed woman rolled her eyes and headed for the motorcycle. Sandra gave her a smile and then put her van in reverse. It was time to get out of Dodge. "Are you buckled up, honey?"

"Yes. You don't always have to ask me that. I always buckle up. The soy milk lady's a dancer?" Joanna sounded horrified.

That's probably a good thing, Sandra thought. She had read that dancing was good for mental health.

"*You* should dance too, Mom."

Sandra laughed so suddenly that she snorted. "Why do you say that, honey?"

"I think you'd be good at it."

"That's sweet of you. But I have no idea how to dance."

"You dance in church!" she chirped.

This was not true. She swayed back and forth in church. This wasn't dancing. "Maybe," she said, thinking about the tornado woman. She felt bad for Joyelle. She had to teach that woman? Sandra hoped she charged more to teach her than she did to teach Joanna. Did the tornado woman throw things at Joyelle too? She realized Joanna was still talking. "What did you say, honey?"

"I said that when you say maybe, it means no. You think we don't know that, but we do."

It was true. Sandra often said no to her children, but sometimes, maybe was easier.

Chapter 5

Apparently devastated that his wife wouldn't have dinner with him, Nate had instead done the brave thing of taking his two sons out to eat. He'd left a note on the fridge that read, "Having a men's night out. Don't wait up."

Sandra laughed, appreciative of the quiet house, and asked Joanna if she wanted to watch a movie.

Joanna's eyes lit up. "Really?"

"Sure. But I get to pick." She couldn't handle any more *My Little Pony*. Nothing against the ponies. She even liked them. But there was such a thing as too many ponies. She poured popcorn kernels into the hot air popper and then put some butter in a saucepan. Leaving her appliances to do their things, she went to the remote control and started searching through movies. Having three children, she'd seen most of the good ones already and the best ones many times. Joanna's addiction to magical ponies had nothing on Peter's Kung Fu Panda fixation. She scrolled past *The Cat in the Hat*, and Joanna squealed.

"Cat in the Hat! Cat in the Hat!"

Sandra groaned.

"Please, Mom? He's so funny!"

Fine. She wasn't going to get to pick after all. She rarely did. She pressed play and then went back to pour the butter on the popcorn and add the nutritional yeast. Some of the popcorn had overshot the bowl and now their female cat, Mr. T, was batting the kernels around on the floor. Sandra decided she'd clean that up later. Let the cat have her fun. The movie was starting. She scooted back into the living room and snuggled in beside her daughter, who rested her head on Sandra's shoulder. She kissed her on the top of her head and then started on the popcorn.

Soon after the popcorn was polished off, Sandra grew drowsy and pulled a blanket up around her shoulders. And then she was out like a light.

She woke, confused as to where and when she was, to her husband shaking her arm. "Why didn't you answer your phone?" he asked accusingly.

She sat up and tried to shake the cobwebs out. "I don't know. I didn't hear it ring?"

"What's the point of paying for that phone if you never have it on?"

"It's on! It's—" Uh oh. As her hand went to her pocket, she knew it was pointless. She clearly remembered plugging the phone into Miss Joyelle's wall.

And then leaving it there.

"I'm sorry, Nate. I forgot it at the dance studio."

He sighed. "Well, I couldn't get the car to start and I needed a boost."

"Sorry," she said again. What did he want from her? She rubbed her eyes. "Did you call a tow truck?"

"Yes. It was either that or walk home."

Sandra glanced at Joanna, who was still riveted by her giant talking cat in the candy cane hat. Sandra pulled the blanket off and stood. Nate was still staring at her.

"What?" she asked.

"Can you go get it?"

"Go get the phone?" She looked at the clock on the wall. "It's too late!"

He didn't say anything.

"The studio will be closed."

"Can you call the studio owner?"

Sandra closed her eyes. She was incredibly tired. "I'm not going to call her in the middle of the night and ask her to make a special trip to the studio because *I* forgot *my* phone."

He frowned. "It's not the middle of the night, and doesn't she *live* at the studio?"

What? "No! Why would she live at the studio?"

It was his turn to look a little chagrined. "I don't know. I assumed she had classes in her basement or something." He rubbed his jaw. "I really don't think we should leave it there overnight. That's an expensive phone."

Yes, and that's why they had insurance on it. She stepped toward him, wanting to make peace. "I will call her first thing in the morning."

He hesitated. "Promise?"

She nodded.

"You won't wake up with fifty other things to do and forget?"

"No, I won't. And even if I did, I'm pretty sure you'd remind me. I promise. First thing tomorrow, before any other crises hit." Even though calling Joyelle in the morning would be only slightly less annoying than calling her now. She stood on her tiptoes and gave her husband a light kiss. "I'm going to bed. Can you tuck Joanna in?" She didn't wait for an answer. She walked past him then and smiled at Peter. "How was dinner?"

"It was awesome. Dad let us have dessert."

"Oh! So it was a special occasion!" Maybe she could convince Nate to have a men's night out every Tuesday.

Chapter 6

Sandra felt incredibly bothersome as she called Joyelle. "So sorry to trouble you. I left my phone in your waiting room last night, and I don't need it back right this second, but I was wondering when the studio would be open again, so I could come get it." She spoke the words as fast as possible, trying not to take up much of Joyelle's valuable time.

Sandra could hear the smile in her voice. "No worries. It happens all the time. I'll go unlock the studio so you can pop in and grab your phone when you're ready."

Really? "Great, thanks! Do you want me to lock it back up when I leave?"

"No, there's no way to do that without a key, but don't worry about it. No one should mess with my studio. There's not much to steal unless someone wants a lifetime collection of Disney soundtracks." She tittered.

Sandra chuckled. "All right. Thank you so much, and sorry about this."

"Like I said, it's nothing to worry about. Stuff like this happens all the time. My older girls spend so much of their time at the studio, they practically live there. You wouldn't believe the treasures I've found left behind!"

Sandra thanked her again and hung up the phone. She told Nate the plan, and he sounded relieved. Joanna asked if she could come. "No, honey. I'll only be gone a few minutes." She practically ran out the door but then paused to enjoy the fresh autumn air. It was so sweet it made her smile, and she had a little bounce in her step as she went to her minivan.

She took the opportunity of being alone to go through the Aroma Joe's drive-through, determined to be as kind as possible to the woman in the window, who turned out to be neither of the tornado woman's victims. Nonetheless, Sandra was as kind as she could be and was rewarded with the most delicious coffee ever. And it didn't even have any soy milk in it.

With her caffeine addiction satiated, she headed for Synergy Dance Studio.

A Lexus was parked in front of the studio door. That was odd. Was someone else there? She got out of the van and went inside. She had an unsettled feeling, like something was wrong. She picked up her phone and charger and then scanned the room. It looked and smelled exactly as it had the night before. The lights were on in the large adjacent room where the dancing took place. Why had Joyelle turned on all the lights? Were they all on one switch? Sandra looked around for a light switch. She should turn them off, try to save Joyelle's electric bill. She found the switch by the door and flipped it down, but only the lights in the lobby went off.

Feeling like a snoop, she stepped into the larger room. Her unsettled feeling grew. The mirrors all along one wall made the room feel huge. Again, Sandra scanned the room for a light switch, and her peripheral vision caught something in the mirror. Her eyes snapped back to the image, her stomach rolled over, and then slowly she slid her eyes away from the reflection and to the sight itself.

A woman wearing Easter-egg-purple leggings lay crumpled against the wall. Sandra's feet didn't want to move, but she insisted. She crossed the room and knelt beside the woman whose very blond hair was now wet with red. Too much red. A dance trophy lay on its side a few feet away from the fallen dancer.

Knowing there was little hope, Sandra pressed two fingers to the woman's neck, but she was cool to the touch.

Sandra stood and backed away. Then she called her favorite State Police detective.

Chip Buker answered on the third ring. "Oh no. What's happened?"

Apparently, his caller ID was working.

"I'm at Synergy Dance Studio in Plainfield. I'm not sure of the address …" She thought for a second. "It's right on Route 27, though. Anyway, I've just found a body. She was hit in the head."

Chip groaned. "Are you safe?"

Her eyes flew around the room. She hadn't really considered that question yet. "I think so? I think it happened a long time ago. She's cool to the touch." Knowing he was going to scold her for touching the woman, she hurried to add, "I only touched her neck to check for a pulse."

"All right. Stay there. Don't touch anything else. I'm on my way."

Sandra hung up on Chip. She had two more calls to make. First, she had to phone Joyelle.

Then she had to call her favorite middle school sports angel, Bob.

Chapter 7

To snoop or not to snoop. That was the question. Sandra had found a dead woman. That did *not* mean she had to try to figure out who had killed her. She could wait until Chip got there and then walk away like a normal person. Part of her brain had already decided that is what she should and would do. But a second part of her brain was calling the first part a liar. *Could* she stay out of it? Did she have that kind of restraint?

She heard sirens and braced herself for the oncoming Slaughter.

Sure enough, Karen Slaughter, wearing her signature black pantsuit, beat Chip through the door. "Did you touch anything?" she snapped.

Sandra didn't want to gratify her with a response, but she thought she should be civil. "I touched her neck to look for a pulse, but that's all."

Chip entered then, along with two other police officers in uniform.

"You didn't touch anything in the room?" Slaughter didn't believe her.

"I did not."

Slaughter snapped on some gloves and then squatted to look at the body as Chip's eyes scanned the room. One of the other officers started taking pictures. Sandra stepped back, taking care not to be in any of them.

Chip also donned gloves and then went to the closest purse.

"That's hers," Sandra said, mostly to herself, but Chip nodded and Slaughter glared at her.

Chip pulled out a Coach wallet and opened it to find a driver's license. "Jazmyn Jecks?" He frowned. "That doesn't even sound like a real name." He straightened and looked at Sandra. "Want to step out with me for a minute? I need to ask you some questions."

Gladly. Though she was more eager to get away from Slaughter than from the dead body on the floor. She followed Chip through the lobby and back out into the wonderful fresh air, thankful that Joanna hadn't come along on this errand.

Chip stopped on the sidewalk and turned to face her, notebook and pen in hand. He raised his eyebrows. Was there a question forthcoming? She waited for one, just in case. "Well?" he said.

"Well what?"

"Tell me the story."

She didn't know where to begin. "My daughter just started dance class for the first time ..." He looked impatient, so she sped up the timeline. "I left my phone here last night. I came here this morning to pick it up. And I found her. That's the whole story. I didn't see anyone else and haven't seen any ..." She didn't want to use the word clues. It was like admitting that she'd snooped.

"Clues?" he offered.

She didn't protest.

"Do you know the victim?"

"I don't. But I saw her buying coffee yesterday. Actually, she was returning coffee at Aroma Joe's ..." He was getting impatient again. "And I could tell from that interaction that she wasn't a pleasant person. Or maybe she was just having a bad day." She doubted the latter explanation. "A *really* bad day. And then I saw her swear at one of the other adult dancers."

"She was an adult dancer?"

Of course she was. Hadn't he seen those leggings? "I made that assumption. She was here last night during the adult class."

He snickered. What could be funny? She scowled at him.

"Sorry, but I didn't realize you were a dancer."

Her scowl deepened. She wasn't, of course, but why would he have such a hard time believing that she was? "I'm not in the class," she said through closed teeth. "As I said, my *daughter* is the dancer, and her class gets out before the adult class."

His smile fell away. "I see. All right, so you didn't know the victim personally?"

"No, but Joyelle did. She should be here any—"

Joyelle's car came into the parking lot on two wheels. She sped into a parking spot, threw the car into park, and was halfway out of the car before she turned the engine off. She wore a sparkly dance team jacket and leggings, making Sandra wonder if she lived in dance clothes.

"What happened?" she cried to no one in particular. On the phone, Sandra had only told her that she'd found a body in her studio. She hadn't tried to explain who it was.

"Are you the owner?" Chip asked.

Joyelle nodded frantically.

Chapter 8

"I'm sorry," Chip said, "but Sandra here found one of your dancers dead in your studio."

Joyelle looked at Sandra with panic in her eyes.

"An *adult* dancer," Sandra said quickly. Still horrific, but she didn't want Joyelle thinking there was a dead child in there.

"Yes, sorry, I should have been more specific. An adult dancer. Sandra identified her purse, and the ID inside the purse belonged to Jazmyn Jecks."

Joyelle's shoulders relaxed. She still looked mortified but less panicked. She nodded slowly and then tipped her head toward the Lexus. "That's Jazmyn's car."

"Was it parked here when you unlocked the studio?" Sandra asked.

"*I'll* ask the questions," Chip said. Then he waited for her to answer Sandra's question.

"I didn't unlock the studio. I asked my son to do it on his way to work. He drives right by."

"Why did you want the studio unlocked?"

Joyelle nodded toward Sandra. "She needed to stop by to pick up her phone." She looked at Jazmyn's car. "She had asked to stay late last night to practice one of her solos." She bit her lip and shook her head.

Then she looked at Chip. "What happened? How did she die?"

"We're still trying to determine that, ma'am," Chip said gently. "Do you need to get anything out of your studio? We need to process it as a crime scene."

Joyelle's head jerked back. "How long will that take?"

Chip shook his head. "Not sure. Shouldn't be too long."

"I hope not because I've got classes starting at four and teams coming in to rehearse at three."

"We will be out of your way as soon as possible. How long have you known Ms. Jecks?"

Joyelle narrowed her eyes. "Someone killed her, didn't they?"

"Why do you say that?" Chip said.

"Because if she died of a heart attack, why would you care how long I've known her?"

"Routine questions, ma'am." He waited for her to answer.

She pinched her temples with one hand. "This is her third year dancing with me."

"And what can you tell me about her?"

"She was a passionate dancer," she said. Her voice had changed, but Sandra didn't know what that change meant.

"And?" Chip pushed.

"And I don't know much else about her."

He gave her a tight smile. "Surely you know more than that."

Joyelle looked at Sandra as if looking for help, but Sandra didn't know what help she needed. And then she remembered the flying coffee and did know. "Are you trying to avoid speaking ill of the dead?"

Joyelle nodded. "Something like that." She looked at Chip. "Are my answers confidential?"

"To an extent. Not entirely."

She sighed, put one hand on her hip, and studied the eaves of her studio. "I'm not sure how to explain it. She was very ... temperamental. She acted more like a four-year-old than the kids in my pre-K class do. She was volatile, explosive ... and she had a very high opinion of herself. She was a good dancer, but she wasn't as good as she thought she was. She wanted to be a star, and she worked hard to be a star, but she wasn't a team player. I don't know. She was a loner, an often unpleasant loner."

39

"Ma'am, that's a *very* good job explaining it. So I'm guessing she had a lot of enemies?"

Joyelle thought about that. "You know, I'm not so sure about that. I don't know as anyone cared about her enough to be her enemy. The women in my class mostly just laughed it all off. Sure, she made them angry, but they would be over it within minutes. So I don't know if she had any real enemies. And I certainly can't think of anyone *who would murder her*." She emphasized the last four words to make it clear that she knew that Jazmyn had, in fact, been murdered.

Chip flipped his notebook shut. "Do you need anything from inside the studio?"

She shook her head slowly. "Not that I can think of."

"Okay. If you think of anything, let one of the officers know. Please don't go in alone. And thank you. You've been very helpful." He gave Sandra a tight-lipped nod and went back inside.

"I'm so sorry," Sandra said because she didn't know what else to say.

Now Joyelle was studying the sidewalk. "I am too. They say there's no such thing as bad publicity, but I'm thinking they're wrong."

Chapter 9

Sandra hadn't wanted to leave the crime scene, but she couldn't think of a valid reason to stick around. And she had to get home to take over Sammy duty, so Nate could get to school. He liked to be there early, so she was already messing with his schedule.

From her front porch, she could hear the chaos inside. Sounded like her family was hosting quite the breakfast bash. She gingerly opened the door, but nothing flew out at her, and she was able to safely enter her house. As she shut the door behind her, Mr. T gave her a dirty look from her perch on the banister. She ran a hand along her back as she walked by her and into the kitchen. "What's going on in here?"

Peter was playing a video game on the television, and the volume was turned up way too loud, so the living room was full of machine gun fire. He'd probably turned it up so he could hear it over Sammy's screaming, but why did he have to hear the game's gunfire at all? Didn't it always sound the same? Sandra scooped a grubby Sammy out of his high chair, and the screaming stopped. "Turn that down!" she called to her eldest.

"Dad burned the toaster strudels!" Joanna cried.

"Tattle-tale," Nate said. He grabbed his bag and travel mug. "Did you find it?"

She nodded.

"Thank you." He kissed her on the cheek. "Gotta go."

"Wait?"

He hesitated, obviously annoyed.

"I'll walk you out."

Looking suspicious, he turned toward the door. "Bye, kids. Love you bunches."

She followed him out onto the porch. "So, I sort of found a dead body at the studio."

He was halfway down the steps, but he stopped, turned, and looked up at her. "You're kidding."

She gave him a look that said obviously she wouldn't kid about that.

He shook his head. "What is it with you? Most people never encounter a murder scene in their whole lives."

She shrugged one shoulder. "I'm special?"

He didn't laugh. "You know I'm going to ask you to stay out of it."

"I haven't done anything yet."

He gave her a small smile. "*Yet*. Exactly. That's the part that concerns me. Who was it?"

"One of the adult students. Jazzy or Jasmine or something like that."

He nodded thoughtfully. "Did you call Bob yet?"

"I said a short prayer. But I didn't make any demands. I just wanted to let him know that it had happened."

Nate sighed. "I really do have to go. Please don't do any snooping till we've had a chance to talk about it? I know I probably can't stop you, but I don't want to spend all day worrying about you."

She nodded. "I can do that."

He turned to go to his car, and she went back inside. The television was still as loud as it had been, if not louder, and she stomped across the living room and turned it off.

"Hey!" Peter cried.

"We have to go to school. Go finish getting ready!"

"I am ready!"

She raised her eyebrows. "Did you brush your teeth?"

His face fell, and he got up and trudged upstairs.

"I brushed my teeth!" Joanna piped up, still picking at a burned toaster strudel.

"Good job, honey. Do you want me to make you another one?"

"This was the last blueberry."

Sandra took Sammy to the sink and started to scrub the blueberry goo off his face. He started screaming again. Her phone rang. She looked down to see who was calling, prepared to let it go to voicemail, but it was her reffing boss. She swiped at the screen to answer the call, but her hand was wet and slippery, so it kept on ringing. She frantically wiped her hands off and then went to try again, but Bob had suddenly appeared in front of her. His hands were dry, so he answered her phone, and then, with a beaming smile, held it out to her.

She took it and put it to her ear. "Hello?" But then she missed most of what the voice on the other end said because Joanna was staring at her open-mouthed, wondering how the phone had just leapt off the countertop, hesitated in midair, and then jumped out toward her mother's hand. "I'm sorry, can you repeat that?" She forced herself to focus on the voice on the phone.

"Today. Dixville Falls. Middle school girls. Four o'clock. Can you do it?"

"Uh, hang on. Let me check the calendar." Again, not thinking about Joanna, she held Sammy out to Bob, so she could use both hands on her phone. She opened the calendar app. "Yes, I can do today at four."

"Great. Thanks."

She hung up and realized that Joanna had pushed her chair back from the table and was pale with fear. Oh no! What had she done? How could she have been so absentminded? She grabbed Sammy out of Bob's invisible arms and rushed to her daughter and knelt beside her chair. "It's okay, honey." She pushed the hair back from her face. "Bob," she said, without looking away from her daughter's wide eyes, "can you please show yourself to her so she won't be so scared?"

Joanna's face instantly relaxed.

"Sorry, Joanna," he said, and there was something beautiful in hearing her daughter's name come from his mouth. "Didn't mean to scare you. Should have thought of that before I tried to help your mom with the phone. I don't usually help people with phones." He smiled.

Joanna smiled back. "You're the angel."

Sandra gasped. "How do you know that?"

Joanna looked at her. "That's Bob. He's your angel friend who helps you find murderers. You guys think I don't hear things, but I do."

Chapter 10

Bob settled into the front seat of the van as if he owned the place.

It was a relief to have everyone in the vehicle aware of his presence. She didn't have to think about pretending that he wasn't there. Lying was so stressful, even when it wasn't technically lying.

She backed out of their driveway and got pointed in the right direction. Once she'd put the van in drive, she said, "There. Now that we have a chance to talk, thanks for coming. I wasn't sure you would."

"You're welcome, but I didn't come because you invited me."

She could hear the smile in his voice, but she glanced at him anyway to confirm it.

"Keep your eyes on the road, Mom!" Peter scolded from the middle seat.

"So then why did you come?"

"The dance angel asked me to."

Sandra laughed. So did Peter.

"There's a dance angel?" Sandra asked.

Bob nodded. "Of course."

"But there's not a specific soccer angel," Peter complained, "so why do dancers get their own angel?"

"Because we're better!" Joanna said, which made little sense, as she also played soccer, though not as enthusiastically as her big brother.

"Dancers," Bob answered, speaking louder as if that could make them be quieter, "have their own angel, but the angel covers a much bigger territory than I do. Anyway ..." He lowered his voice again. "The owner of the studio is *very* shaken up, and—"

"Understandably," Sandra interrupted.

"Yes. Understandably. She's worried that her reputation will be damaged. And it is a stellar one. Untarnished. And she's worried that her young dancers will be scared to come to class. Her studio is supposed to be a place of joy and safety, not a place where children think about murdered corpses."

Sandra shuddered at the thought.

"So she's been praying for help, which the dance angel is willing to give. But because I've sort of got a reputation now for being something of a sleuth, he asked me if I'd help."

Sandra snickered. "Is he going to help too?"

"Of course he's willing if we need him. But I don't think we will."

Sandra got the sense Bob didn't *want* the dance angel to help. Maybe he wanted to be the only sleuthing angel. "What's this dance angel's name?"

Bob hesitated. "I'm probably not supposed to tell you that."

Bummer. She liked angel names, even if she couldn't pronounce them.

"Anyway, I told him I would help. I owe him one. He saved my hide a few centuries ago, and I'm happy to have a chance to return the favor."

The idea of being alive for centuries made Sandra's head spin. She glanced at him again. "You look good for a guy several centuries old."

"Try millennia. Anyway, it's my turn to ask you for help."

"Me?"

"Yes, you. Don't get an inflated sense of yourself. I don't have a lot of options for human sleuthing partners."

"I would help you!" Peter said.

"Let's hope you don't have to this time," Sandra said, though she was a little proud of her son for volunteering.

They rode in silence for a minute. "You say she's praying about her reputation and her children's fears ... but she isn't worried about the killer coming back?"

He thought about that for a few seconds. "I don't know. Macholyadah didn't mention that."

Aha! She'd gotten an angel name after all. Bob didn't seem to realize he'd slipped, though, so she wasn't going to mention it. "Seems odd to me that she's not worried about the safety of her dancers."

Bob looked at her. "You think *Joyelle* might be the killer?"

No, she didn't think that. Did she? She couldn't imagine Joyelle hurting anyone or anything. "No. I do not think she's the killer. But maybe she knows who *is*."

"And?" he pressed.

Sandra sighed as she pulled the minivan into the long line of cars waiting to offload offspring. "I'm thinking that she knows who the killer is, knows he or she isn't a threat to her students, and, therefore, isn't worried about their safety. If she *didn't* know who the killer was, wouldn't she be scared of a repeat performance?"

"See," Bob said, contemplatively, "I hadn't thought of that. That's why I need your help."

She basked in the praise. "Thank you."

They were quiet for a few minutes, inching the van along one car length at a time.

"If Joyelle already knows who the killer is," Bob said, "then maybe we don't need to go looking for him. Maybe we just need to get closer to Joyelle, get her to tell you who he is."

"Maybe!" She wouldn't mind getting closer to Joyelle. The woman was wonderful. "And that won't be hard as I will already be hanging around because of Joanna's dance class."

"No," Bob said quickly. "That won't be close enough."

She looked at him. "What do you mean?"

"I mean you need to get closer."

"You want me to invite her out for coffee or something?"

He shook his head. "Closer."

She didn't understand. Did he want her to move into the woman's house?

"He wants you to join the adult dance class, Mom," Peter said.

She looked at Bob wide-eyed, and he was grinning. "No."

"Oh yes."

Her heart rate increased. "No."

"Please?"

She gripped the wheel tighter. Hadn't she been tempted by this very idea the day before? But now she was terrified. And she wasn't scared of the killer. She was scared of making a fool of herself. Quietly, she asked, "Can the dance angel make me a better dancer?"

Bob snickered. "I'm sure he *can*. I doubt he *will*. But you won't need his help for that. You'll be fine. All humans can dance. It's a gift from God. Joyelle will take that natural gift and help you shape it into something you'll be proud of."

It was a lovely thought. It didn't quite convince her, though. They had arrived at the front of the line. "Okay, kids!"

Joanna ripped the sliding door open and jumped out. "Bye, Mom! Bye, Sammy! Bye, Bob!" she said loudly and then turned and ran to the door.

Peter climbed out more slowly. "Bye, Mom! Bye, Sammy!" he said at a normal volume. Then he whispered, "Bye, Bob!" and slammed the door shut.

Sandra exhaled heavily, checked her side mirror, and eased the van out of the line.

"Your children are quite spectacular," Bob mused.

"Yes, I know. Thank you."

He snickered.

"What's so funny?"

"I was enjoying your utter lack of humility."

"Humility?" she cried, pulling out onto the main road. "Oh trust me, I wasn't being prideful. I can take no credit for how spectacular my children are. They are gifts from God. Their spectacularness doesn't come from me, and, therefore, I can admire it right along with you."

"Point taken. So, you'll dance?"

She groaned. "I don't know if I can dance." Her brain flickered back through her small collection of embarrassing bridesmaid dance fiascoes. "But maybe I'll try."

Chapter 11

Sandra checked the clock on her minivan's dashboard. She was running late. Refs were supposed to be on the soccer field a half hour before the game started, and she didn't think she was going to make it. But she was partnered with her favorite ref today. Moose was always on time, and he would cover for her if someone needed something. Still, she applied a little more pressure to the accelerator.

Before she'd left the house, she had emailed Joyelle and asked if she could take her up on her mom-and-daughter-dance offer after all. Joyelle had responded immediately. She was overjoyed. Her excitement made Sandra feel guilty. She had no intention of dancing all year and then performing in the recital. She would just dance until she figured out who had killed the Jazzy-soy-milk-woman. She thought she could get that done long before spring recital.

She had almost reached Philip A. Stucker Middle School when she saw the flashing blue lights in her rearview. Her stomach sank, and her heart started hammering. She pulled her minivan onto the shoulder. She didn't know if the blue lights were meant for her, but there was a good chance.

Yep. They'd been meant for her. She swallowed hard. She *hated* getting in trouble. That feeling was worse than any fine they could impose. She waited as the seconds crawled by. The deputy was in no hurry. She kept glancing at the clock, feeling guiltier and guiltier about leaving Moose stranded there on a middle school soccer field. Plus, glancing at the clock kept her from seeing all those staring eyes from passersby.

Finally, he got out of the car. Slowly, he strolled her way. "Good afternoon," he said when he reached the window. Then he smirked. "Nice shirt."

She knew what shirt she was wearing, but for some reason, she looked down anyway. "Thanks. I'm a soccer ref. They make me wear neon."

He nodded. "Sorry about that. You late for a game?"

"Yes, and I'm sorry. I know that's no excuse for speeding—"

"No, it's not."

She knew that. Hadn't she just said that?

"But I'll let you get going so the kids can start their game. But this is a warning. Don't let me catch you speeding again!"

She bobbed her head up and down. "I won't. Thank you so much."

His brow furrowed. "Hey, are you that soccer ref who helped to catch the other soccer ref last fall? The drug dealer?"

Had he really recognized her? Or had he only realized he was staring down at a female soccer ref? There weren't many of those floating around, so maybe this was the one. Sandra wasn't sure how to respond. Cops didn't usually like amateur snoops, right? Maybe he'd change his mind and give her a ticket after all. She swallowed hard. "Yes, that was me."

He laughed and rested a hand on her door. "That was quite an ordeal. Glad you made it out okay."

Phew! He wasn't mad. "Yep. Me too."

"Hey, uh ..." He looked over her hood, staring into the trees. She almost followed his gaze, but she knew there was nothing there. He lowered his voice, "Did you hear about the killing in Plainfield yesterday?"

Yes, she'd heard about it. She'd found the body. "Yes. Very sad."

He nodded. "You planning to do some snooping?" He said this with hope in his voice. He wasn't scolding her. He sounded intrigued, as if he wanted the inside scoop. Maybe he felt left out because he worked for the sheriff's department, and the State Police covered murder investigations in Franklin County, leaving the tiny sheriff's department out of it.

"Well ..." How on earth was she supposed to respond to this? "I don't know about snooping, but my daughter does dance at that school, so—"

"Aha!" He slapped his hand down on her door, grinning ear to ear. "I knew it!" He tipped his head back and laughed. Then he slapped her door again. "Well, you get to that soccer game safely. And if you *do* decide to do some snooping," he said conspiratorially, "you do so *safely*. Don't need any more close calls." He stepped back from her car. "Go on now, get out of here," he said as if she'd been the one lallygagging.

"Will do," she said, putting the van in drive. "Thanks again, Deputy."

He nodded, looking proud and happy, and she drove away, paying hyper-close attention to her speedometer. At least he enjoys his job, she thought. Not everyone could say that.

Chapter 12

She reached the field just as Moose was flipping the coin. She joined him in the captain's circle as swiftly as she could without making it glaringly obvious that she was late. A woman in neon yellow sprinting across the field tended to get people's attention. She apologized under her breath, and Moose flashed her a gentle smile that said, *No worries*.

As the game got going, she fell into the rhythm of it and started to have fun. In all her rushing, she hadn't really noticed what a beautiful day it was. Perfect soccer weather. Not too hot, not too cold, not too windy. The air smelled like autumn with that special soccer scent that she was sure didn't exist anywhere else—the smell of freshly cut grass mixed with raked leaves mixed with sweaty shin guards. With the exception of one overly zealous mother ringing an obnoxiously loud cowbell every time her daughter did something she approved of, the first half was fairly uneventful. She missed a few calls, but she made some good ones too. Her reffing improved with every game, as did her confidence.

Before she knew it, it was halftime, and she jogged over to join Moose in front of the score table.

"Don't you live in Plainfield?" Moose asked after taking a long haul off his water bottle.

She nodded. He knew that she did. Every ref knew where every other ref lived because of carpooling.

"So then you must have heard about the killing?"

She nodded again.

He waited for her to say more, but she didn't. She didn't really know what he wanted her to say, and she wanted to use her mouth to drink her water.

"Are you planning to investigate?"

She laughed, and water almost came out her nose. She coughed and wiped at her mouth. "Investigate?"

He folded his arms over his round belly. "Oh come on, don't act like you quit snooping once you caught Mike White. I know you've turned into some sort of P.I. We all heard about you pulling that guy out of the pond over in the mountains."

She was a little disappointed that he hadn't also heard that she'd helped catch the Cat Vac Villain, but she wasn't going to bring it up.

She didn't want to brag. "I know, Moose, but I don't do these things on purpose." At least, she didn't think she did. Did she? She wasn't sure. "Well, maybe I do, a little, but I don't go seeking them out. I just sort of … stumble onto them." She purposefully didn't answer his question. She didn't want to admit her plans, and she didn't want to lie.

"I s'pose that could be true. It does seem like we've had a lot of murders lately. Too many for rural Maine."

They finished their waters in silence. Then the buzzer sounded, and Moose started toward the circle. She smiled as she watched him go. She couldn't believe how many people just assumed she would be getting involved in this case. Her husband, some random deputy, and now Moose? She hoped Joyelle wouldn't make the same assumption. It would be a lot harder to try to coax information out of her if she knew she was being coaxed.

The second half began much as the first half had ended, and Sandra's legs grew tired. These two teams were evenly matched, which meant a lot of running. She liked those lopsided games where one team simply pounded on the other team's goal, and she basically got to stand still.

They'd switched sides, and Moose was now the one running up and down in front of Ms. Cowbell. Sandra didn't miss her. She'd figured out which child belonged to the overly enthusiastic mom. Number twenty-seven. She was a good player. She was quick, agile, and skilled. But her melodramatic facial expressions kept her play from being admirable. It seemed she was more interested in an Oscar than a soccer trophy. Sandra told herself to be patient, that she was a middle school girl, and it wasn't easy being a middle school girl—especially a middle school girl with a mom armed with a cowbell. Still, if that girl aimed one of her eye rolls at Sandra, the yellow card was coming out.

Not long after she'd promised herself this little treat, number twenty-seven dribbled into the penalty box. Thinking she was probably going to get a shot off, Sandra sprinted ahead to get a better look. But then, out of nowhere, an equally quick, agile, and skilled defender swept in and stole the ball. It was a beautiful move, and she managed to do it without contorting her face into some farcical expression *and* without touching her opponent.

Yet number twenty-seven flew forward through the air, her arms outstretched, her perfect little perky blond ponytail flying out behind her and then face-planted at the goalkeeper's feet.

Moose did not blow the whistle. The skilled sweeper continued to dribble the ball up the field, and Moose followed her.

But number twenty-seven was not happy. She slowly got to her feet, her eyes huge and her mouth open, and she turned to look at her mother, who had gotten to her feet. Uh oh. Sandra's stomach turned, and she quickly turned away from the spectacle, pretending she wasn't aware of it. She too followed the sweeper. And Ms. Cowbell started screaming. Sandra sprinted away from them, in part because she was out of position and in part because she was desperate to get away from those two.

She wished the rest of the game would take place on the other end of the field.

And then the cowbell started ringing.

Chapter 13

A goal from number twenty-seven's team usually got a cowbell salute of about four shakes. "*Dong-dong, dong-dong, dong-dong, dong-dong,*" and then she was done. A good move by her daughter, two or three good shakes.

This was something else. This was a steady *DONG-DONG-DONG-DONG* with no letting up. Sandra wouldn't let herself look back, but it was obvious that the woman was pumping that bell for all it was worth, and it was *so loud*. Sandra grew less fearful and more annoyed. It had been the right call. That sweeper hadn't touched her daughter. That little girl had faked falling down so she could get the trip call, and Sandra was sure that everyone on the field knew it—everyone, that is, but Ms. Cowbell.

The ball was batted back and forth by players in the other eighteen, and Sandra tried to concentrate on the game, but ... was the cowbell getting *louder*? She glanced at Moose, but he was doing a great job of pretending he couldn't hear it. Or maybe he really couldn't. She'd heard that refs developed selective hearing. And then eventually a loss of hearing.

No, she decided. No way could selective hearing filter that obnoxious ringing out. It was *so loud*. It was all she could do not to turn back and look, and several of the players had done just that. They'd stopped moving and were staring at what was happening behind her. Sandra glanced at their faces and didn't like what she saw.

They looked scared.

Sandra looked at Moose, who was still watching the ball.

Ms. Cowbell started to scream, and nearly every other word was an obscenity. Her voice made Sandra long for a thousand fingernails on a thousand chalkboards. Still, she didn't look. One by one, the players stopped playing and turned toward the spectacle.

Was the cowbell getting louder? Was the cowbell getting *closer?*

She didn't look.

Neither did Moose.

There was a breakaway, and a girl dribbled alone toward the goal. The goalkeeper didn't even look at her. Sandra, realizing she was supposed to be on the goal line, started to sprint, but before she could even get going, a blur of pink flashed through her peripheral vision.

She couldn't stand it anymore. She looked. A fluffy mom with giant blond hair was running at Moose. Above her head and slightly out in front of her, she rang a cowbell.

Sandra froze. "Mooooose!" she hollered with all her might.

Finally, he looked. His feet stopped moving, his jaw dropped open, and the whistle fell out of his mouth.

Sandra didn't know what to do. What was happening? Was Ms. Cowbell going to assault him? Yes, yes, it appeared she was. But was she going to assault him with her vile language alone? Or did she plan to use the cowbell?

Sandra scanned the touchline for the school's athletic director, but she didn't see her. The home coach looked horrified. The visiting coach had his hand over his mouth to hide his laughter, but the fact that his whole body was jiggling betrayed the truth.

Sandra turned back to look at Moose who was backpedaling away from the bell-wielding mother. But she was gaining on him. She pulled her hand back, and it became clear that she was actually going to hit him. This spurred Sandra into action. She had to help Moose! She turned toward the home coach and hollered, "Find your A. D." Then she ran toward the conflict, shouting for the woman to stop.

The woman swung, but Moose dodged the blow. He was still backpedaling as he did so, and this made for an awful, awkward balance-disturbing twist. He stumbled and fell backward. Down he went, onto his rump, and the woman pulled back to hit him again, even though he was on the ground. Sandra pushed herself to get there in time and then lunged. As Moose used his hands to slide back away from her, Sandra grabbed her arm.

Ms. Cowbell turned to look at Sandra. Her eyes were huge and wild, and gave Sandra a chill. It seemed the woman had only just realized that Sandra was on the field.

"Never mind, Sandra!" Moose had pulled himself to his feet and was starting to run away—toward the parking lot.

Sandra let go of the woman's arm and backed away from her, but now the woman was coming for her, with cowbell raised and cusses spewing.

"Sandra! Come on!" Moose's voice sounded unrealistically far away.

Was he leaving the field? She considered her options. She could try for the school, but it might be locked, and the parking lot was closer. She could try for the snack shack, but then what? She'd be trapped in the snack shack. And the snack shack booster was probably Ms. Cowbell's cousin or sister-in-law or dental hygienist.

She turned toward the parking lot and ran. She ran so fast that her shirt flapped out behind her, cooling the sweat from her back. She was confident she could outrun Ms. Cowbell, and the relief of being free of her was sweet. She caught her reffing partner just as his cleats clopped onto the hard asphalt of the parking lot. He ripped his truck door open and threw himself behind the wheel.

She stopped running and turned to look behind her.

The woman was still coming.

Moose laid on his truck horn, which jumped the tar out of her. As if her heart hadn't already been beating fast enough.

"Get in!" he hollered through the windshield.

She hurried around to the passenger door. She probably didn't need to hurry. Ms. Cowbell was huffing and puffing and no longer brandishing her weapon over her head. Instead, it hung limply at her side. But Sandra hurried, nonetheless. She sensed her hurrying was important to Moose. Sure enough, as soon as she shut the door, he threw the truck into reverse and peeled out.

She put her hand in her head, embarrassed. The other refs were going to be talking about this for years. As he continued backing up at a breakneck speed, she looked out the windshield to see that Ms. Cowbell had stopped. She was bent over, her hands on her knees, breathing hard. Sandra knew the feeling.

Moose slammed on the brakes and put the truck in drive.

Sandra looked at the sky, searching for some sign of Bob. Wasn't this situation exactly what he was there for? To defend innocent referees from murderous cowbell-brandishing mothers?

Moose slammed on the brakes again and looked up and down the road. Seeing no other vehicles, he yanked the truck out onto the road.

"Where are we going?" she said, stretching one arm out to steady herself on the dusty dashboard.

"We are going to Burger King."

She snorted. "Burger King? Why?"

"Because I'm hungry. And we need to give her time to go home. Then we'll come back for our bags, and if it's safe, you can get in your own car."

She fell quiet. She was pretty sure that the closest Burger King was in Lewiston. This was twenty minutes away. She didn't want to go to Lewiston or to Burger King, but she didn't have a better plan. "I guess Burger King makes a fine hideout."

Moose grunted. "This ain't my first rodeo."

Sandra wondered if Burger King still had a rodeo burger and smiled.

"What's so funny?"

"Nothing."

A smile crept onto Moose's face. "Okay, it was a little funny. But we could choose not to tell people."

"Are you serious? We need to report that!"

Moose rubbed his jaw and glanced into the rearview mirror nervously. "All right. But can we leave out the part where I fell on my keister?"

Sandra laughed. "Sure."

"And I don't know about you, but I'm blocking all future games for that school. I've been saying I was going to do that for years, but I've blocked so many schools now, I don't have many left."

Sandra laughed again. "We can wait for her child to get to high school, then we can unblock the school again."

He nodded. "If I remember."

"That wasn't a trip, by the way," she said, referring to the call Ms. Cowbell had accused him of missing.

"I know it wasn't. Little Miss Twenty-Seven was faking it. Like I said—"

"Not your first rodeo. I know, I know."

"It's worse than you think. That child is the third daughter in that family. You should see the oldest. She's a senior."

Sandra was so glad she never reffed varsity games.

"I'm really hoping there aren't any more kids in that family."

Chapter 14

At first, Sandra had been so motivated to help Bob figure out who had killed Jazmyn. And if good intentions did anything, she would already have the crime all solved. But that's not the way things were going. The week had slipped by, frantic minute by frantic minute. She'd had to zip kids back and forth to soccer practice. She'd had two more games herself, games for which she was grateful, as she'd wondered if the whole Dixville Falls debacle would lead to her termination. Instead, her boss had dealt sternly with the Dixville Falls athletic director.

In addition to all the demands of soccer season, she'd had to last-second-prepare for, then facilitate, and then clean up after a knitting workshop at church. This was more of an ordeal than it should have been as she wasn't a very good knitter, and she was incredibly stressed out about the whole affair. She was sure that there were real, expert knitters in the group waiting to judge her.

Somehow, Tuesday afternoon sneaked up and then popped out at her like a scary clown out of a jack-in-the-box. Dance night. It was time for Joanna's dance class, which wasn't very scary at all. But it was time for hers.

She had nothing to wear.

"Just wear some sweatpants," Nate suggested less than helpfully. She thought back to what the other women had been wearing. She couldn't remember any sweatpants. Colorful leggings and flowing sleeveless tops. One woman in leather shorts and black fingerless fishnet gloves that reached past her elbows. One woman who looked as though she'd just stepped off the plane from India. One woman in an olive jumpsuit. But no sweatpants.

"I can't wear sweatpants," she snapped.

He looked wounded.

"Sorry, I'm just stressed out." More like panicked.

"Wear your reffing outfit," Peter said with a snort, and she threatened to ground him for the rest of his life.

"Let's go shopping," Joanna chirped.

"We don't have time," Sandra said. Nor did they have extra money to spend on Mommy dance clothes. She announced that Mommy needed a time out and asked her children to please stay downstairs. Then she went upstairs to contend with her options.

She opened the closet door and surveyed the options.

Then she went through her drawers.

Sweatpants it is, she thought. She pulled her "newest" pair out of the bottom drawer. She'd bought them used before Joanna was born. She shook them out and then promptly sneezed. She'd left the drawer open a few inches, and Mr. T had squirmed in there for a nap or two. Maybe three. Now her black sweatpants were mostly white. She gave them another firm shake and then put them on. At least they were comfortable. She then pulled a faded Tenth Avenue North T-shirt out of her drawer and on over her head. She put her hair up in a sort-of-bun, looked in the mirror, flinched, and then headed for the door.

Nate met her in the hallway. He wrapped her in his arms and kissed her on top of the head. "You look lovely," he said, managing to sound sincere. He stepped back and held her at arm's length.

"Thank you," she mumbled.

He let out a long breath. "I'm still not excited that you're doing this, but I appreciate your braveness. Just remember, no investigating unless Bob is *right there.*"

"I've already promised that." She had to get going. They were going to be late. She tried to get by him, but he didn't let go of her.

"I know that. Promise me again?"

Something in his tone softened her heart and calmed her spirit. She smiled up at him. "I promise." She brushed her lips against his and then pulled away. "Gotta go!"

She herded Joanna into the van and then headed toward Synergy Dance Studio.

"Where's Bob?" Joanna chirped from the back.

Sandra had been thinking the same thing ever since Ms. Cowbell had threatened to kill her with the world's most obnoxious murder weapon. She looked in the rearview mirror. "Joanna?"

She looked up, and she was so adorable in her little leotard.

"*I* know that I'm helping Bob, and *you* know that I'm helping Bob, but no one else can know that, right?"

She nodded eagerly and put her small finger up to her lips. "It's a secret, I know."

"Good girl. We don't want Bob getting in trouble with God, so we have to keep him a secret."

"I know. I won't tell anyone."

"And we can't tell anyone that I'm trying to figure out who hurt that woman. That's a secret too."

Joanna tipped her head to the side and gave Sandra an exasperated look. "I *know* that, Mom. I'm not stupid." She sounded more like a fourteen-year-old than an eight-year-old.

"Slow this life down, Father," Sandra prayed under breath. "Slow us down."

Chapter 15

Feeling like she might be sick, Sandra stepped into the studio for her turn. She tried to be invisible as she tiptoed to the corner of the room.

She watched the women as they came into the large room. They all wore shiny black tap shoes, so it was easy to be quiet and feel invisible in all that clickety chaos. The supermodel who looked like a Barbie doll had already been in the room when she'd entered. She was talking to Joyelle in the front of the room. Whatever they were talking about, they were very hush-hush, and Sandra strained to eavesdrop without looking at them.

The very pregnant woman entered soon after Sandra did. She wobbled to the center of the room and then sat down to stretch out. Sandra was amazed at how flexible she was, given her condition. Next came the Bluetooth woman. She'd changed out of her pantsuit, but she was still chattering away on her earpiece. She also sat down on the floor and started stretching.

Oh, was that what they were supposed to be doing? Sandra grabbed hold of the bar on the wall beside her and pulled her heel to her butt. Her knee screamed in protest. This stretch would be easier on her aging joints if she lay down to do it, but she didn't want to do that because she was still considering making a run for it. Next through the door came a petite woman with mouse-brown hair. She looked at the floor as she walked, and even though she wore tap shoes like everyone else, they barely made a sound.

Next came the motorcycle woman, who made a beeline for Sandra. Sandra stiffened as she approached. She extended her hand. "Name is Jess!" Her high-pitched, cheerful voice did not match her copious black eyeliner. "Welcome!"

Sandra accepted the handshake and instantly felt more relaxed. "Thank you. My name is Sandra."

Jess pivoted away from her so she had room to stretch. "I know! Joyelle is very excited you've decided to join us. I saw your little cutie in the last class. Joyelle just loves her to pieces."

Already? That was a good sign. "I do too."

Joyelle got everyone's attention and welcomed them warmly. "We're going to start with some basic techniques. They might feel a little tricky if they are new to you, but don't worry. Soon they'll be second nature." She turned and faced the mirror, and the women spread out evenly into lines.

Joyelle started moving her feet. "This is called a scuffle. It's heel, toe, step … heel, toe, step. Just do what I do. Follow my feet."

Sandra started following her and, shockingly, was able to do what Joyelle was telling her to do. It wasn't graceful, but she was doing it! Something inside her leapt a little. This was almost fun!

"Great job, everyone! Now we're going to add to it!" She sounded so excited. "This is called a paradiddle! Start with your scuffle, but instead of stepping, you're going to dig it, and then put your heel down." Sandra didn't know what this meant, but Joyelle demonstrated slowly, and Sandra tried to imitate her. She was really grateful that she wasn't wearing tap shoes because her feet were not doing what everyone else's feet were doing. Everyone else was in perfect unison, making a lovely "*boom, slap, tap, boom … boom, slap, tap, boom …*" It was beautiful and fun, and on the fifth or sixth try, Sandra finally managed to get it. "Great job!" Joyelle said again. Boy, she was some enthusiastic. Yet, she seemed completely sincere. "Who wants to try it a little bit faster?"

Oh no.

"Here we go!"

"Hello?" someone croaked from the doorway.

Joyelle stopped and turned to face the newcomer, as did most of the women in the room.

The stout woman in the doorway leaned on a walker. She wore a bright green romper that matched the tennis balls on the bottom of her walker and somehow complemented her orange hair. She only wore one sock. It was black, pulled up to her knee, and sported a collection of white hairs that made Sandra felt better about her pants.

"Can I help you?" Joyelle asked sweetly.

"I'm Gertrude!"

Chapter 16

It appeared that Joyelle had no idea who Gertrude was, but she was gracious, nonetheless. "Are you here to join the class?"

Gertrude looked around as if she wasn't quite sure of the answer to that question. "I guess so," she said, as if Joyelle was twisting her arm.

"Great! Welcome aboard!" Joyelle swept an arm across the room. "Go ahead and find a spot. We're glad you're here!"

Sandra had a feeling Joyelle might soon be less glad. This woman looked a little grumpy.

Slowly, the newest member of the world's most eclectic dance class pushed her walker across the back of the room. She narrowed her eyes at Sandra as she approached. Sandra didn't know why she was doing this. She didn't know this woman and couldn't imagine how she had offended her already. She forced a smile, trying to appear friendly.

Gertrude pivoted and faced the front of the room. She gave Joyelle a solemn nod as if to say, "You may begin now," and Sandra had to bite back a laugh.

Discreetly, she studied the woman. She moved as if she'd made quite a few trips around the sun, but she looked fairly young. Just how old was she?

Joyelle went back to her teaching, and the class followed her taps, brushes, and stomps. The newcomer, however, made no attempt to follow her. Sandra tried, but she was mighty distracted by her new neighbor, who stood leaning on her walker, studying each of the dancers one by one.

Suddenly, Sandra knew what she was up to. Being a snoop herself, she recognized the signs. This woman was sleuthing! Sort of. She was doing her own version of sleuthing. Her head snapped toward Sandra, and she narrowed her eyes again. Sandra quickly turned to watch herself in the mirror and found Joyelle staring at her—probably wondering why she wasn't following along anymore. Sandra tried to concentrate and be a good student.

Before she knew it, the tap class gave way to jazz, and the women clap-clapped their way out of the room to change their shoes. Sandra, of course, had no shoes to change into or out of. Neither, apparently, did Gertrude. She was wearing white sneakers.

Gertrude caught Sandra staring at her feet.

"Hi. I'm Sandra."

"Gertrude."

"Pleased to meet you."

Joyelle approached then and showed Gertrude some paperwork. It appeared Gertrude wasn't listening to her, though, and when Joyelle finished her sentence, Gertrude shoved the papers into an already swollen walker pouch, crumpling them in the process.

"I won't be here long," Gertrude said, in response to Joyelle's sharing of the class costs. "I'm just here to catch a killer, and then I'll be on my way."

Joyelle raised an eyebrow. "I'm sorry?"

"Did you kill Jazmyn Jecks?" Gertrude asked point-blank.

Sandra was so shocked that she laughed, but Gertrude ignored her.

Joyelle didn't find it funny. "Of course not!"

Gertrude leaned toward Joyelle as if trying to get a better look.

Understandably, Joyelle recoiled.

"I believe you," Gertrude said after a moment of study.

"Thank you?" Joyelle said.

The other women started to filter back into the studio.

"But if you're going to be in the studio, I'll still need to charge you for the class," she tried.

Gertrude ignored her. She was staring at Jess and the woman she was walking with. "That woman is awfully fluffy to be a dancer!"

Sandra's face got hot. The woman beside Jess glared at Gertrude. "You're not exactly a size six yourself."

This was true.

"I'm not exactly going to dance," Gertrude said.

The angry woman gracefully stormed in their direction. "It just so happens that Joyelle welcomes *all* dancers, no matter their color, size, or anything else. She gives *everyone* the gift of dance." The woman stopped and looked Gertrude up and down. "Even you." Her point landed, and she spun on one foot to walk away.

"What's your name?" Gertrude asked her back.

Slowly, the woman turned around.

Sandra folded her arms across her chest, a little upset with herself that this oddball was doing a better job at her job than she was. She'd been asked *by an angel*, and yet she was letting this woman out-sleuth her.

"Astrid."

"Astrid?" Gertrude cried, incredulous. "What kind of name is Astrid?"

"It means divine beauty. It's a name given to royalty."

Gertrude snickered. "Did you kill Jazmyn Jecks?"

Astrid gasped appropriately. "Of course not! I couldn't hurt a flea!"

Gertrude's face twisted up into a scowl. "*Anyone* can hurt a flea, Astrid. They are very small. Not very tough. Did you know Jazmyn?"

"Of course. We all knew her."

Joyelle clapped her hands. "All right. Let's get back to dancing!"

Gertrude ignored the call to order. "Were you friends with her?"

"No," Astrid said quickly.

"I see," Gertrude said thoughtfully.

Astrid rolled her eyes. "None of us were friends with her! Doesn't mean we killed her. Doesn't mean anything at all."

Gertrude chewed her lip. "Interesting use of the word *we.*"

"What?" Astrid asked.

"You said *we* didn't kill her. I never said you all did it." She looked around the room, then back to Astrid. "But it's interesting that you jumped right to that."

Was it? Was that interesting? Sandra wasn't sure, and she didn't like not being sure. She thought this woman was ridiculous, but had she just unearthed a clue?

"Come on, everybody," Jess said. "Joyelle's ready to start." She gave Gertrude a small sideways smile. "You can ask all the questions you want after class."

Gertrude's face fell in disappointment, but she stopped talking. She stood quietly in the back of the room for thirty minutes. As everyone danced around her, she leaned on her walker and studied the room.

Chapter 17

At the end of jazz class, Gertrude followed the supermodel into the waiting room and to her water bottle. Trying to be discreet, Sandra followed.

"What's your name?" Gertrude demanded.

The woman took a long drink. "April." She gave Gertrude a beautiful smile.

"Hi, April. Did you kill Jazmyn?"

Sandra was certain that a woman with a smile that sweet was not a murderer.

April focused on screwing the top back onto her bottle and then put her hands on her hips. "Gertrude, I can promise you that none of Joyelle's students killed Jazmyn. Now, why do you think one of us did?"

Gertrude pursed her lips. "I'm asking the questions!"

April's eyebrows flicked up in surprise, but she kept smiling. "Okay, but *why* are you asking the questions?"

People were quiet, watching the scene unfold while pretending they weren't. Again, Sandra felt she was being outsleuthed. Who *was* this woman?

Gertrude stepped back a foot and then slid her walker back as well. She seemed surprised by the question. She looked around at all the eyes watching her and those that pretended they weren't. "I'm Gertrude, Gumshoe. This is what I do. I catch killers." Her eyes landed on Sandra's. "I'm surprised you've never heard of me."

A few of the women laughed.

Gertrude's eyes grew wide. "Remember that woman who got killed in the Mattawooptock Goodwill? I'm the one who found the murder weapon! And I'm the one who figured out who killed her!"

The laughter grew, as did Gertrude's indignation.

"I'm the one who caught that woman who kidnapped those other women!"

Wow, that was specific. Even more laughter.

"And that dead guy they found at Gunslinger City? I caught that killer too!"

Nearly everyone was laughing now, everyone except for the petite woman with mousy hair. She was still in the studio, peeking out at them. Sandra could tell that the laughter was hurting Gertrude's feelings, and she felt for her. She stepped toward her and said quietly, "Heroes are quickly forgotten."

Gertrude's expression softened—a little.

Sandra nodded toward the woman still in the studio, and the woman ducked out of sight. "Come on. I think you should go question someone over here."

Gertrude looked that way and then back at Sandra suspiciously. "What? You're helping me?"

Not really, Sandra thought. She wanted to ask questions too, but it was easier to let Gertrude do it in her brash, disruptive way. Easier and quicker. "Yes, I'm helping you. Come on." She walked back into the studio, and Gertrude followed.

The woman stood in a corner as if trying to hide from them.

Gertrude stopped walking, looked at Sandra, and clicked her tongue. "Oh yes. She *does* look suspicious." She plodded across the room and then stopped in front of the woman. "What's your name?"

"Mandi, and no, I didn't kill Jazmyn." Her voice was barely audible. "I liked her."

Seriously? Sandra couldn't imagine anyone liking that woman.

"No, you didn't," Gertrude said.

Mandi's eyes grew wet, but she didn't argue.

The women spilled into the room. Sandra didn't know if they were returning for class or if they wanted to watch Gertrude's investigation.

"Why didn't you like her?" Gertrude pressed.

Mandi's head gave a firm, quick shake. "I told you. I *did* like her."

"And I said you didn't. And I'm asking why not. You might as well tell me now before things get worse."

Before things got worse? What did that mean? Was that some weird threat? Or a prediction?

Didn't matter what it was. It held no power over Mandi. Still looking terrified, she stepped sideways and slid along the wall, away from Gertrude. When she'd created a bit of a buffer, she left the wall and returned to her spot at the front of the class.

Gertrude looked at Sandra. "Something suspicious about that one."

Sandra wasn't so sure. Most people didn't want to bad-mouth the dead. If Mandi was lying about liking Jazmyn, Sandra understood why. She left Gertrude then and returned to her spot in the back, hoping Gertrude wouldn't follow.

She got her wish. When she turned to face the mirror, she saw that Gertrude had stayed on the other side of the room and was now questioning the Bluetooth woman. Now Sandra was kicking herself because she couldn't hear what they were saying.

But if Bluetooth woman confessed, she didn't have time to give many details because Joyelle began to teach the lyrical ballet lesson.

Chapter 18

"What do you make of Gertrude?" Bob asked.

Sandra let out a little cry and nearly drove her minivan into a tree.

Joanna giggled. "Hi, Bob."

Without looking back at her, he said, "Hi, punkin. Sorry, didn't mean to startle you."

Sandra wondered if this was true. It seemed he enjoyed startling her. "Where have you been?"

"I'm an angel. I've been busy ministering to the saints."

She bit back a laugh.

"So, how was it?" He sounded impatient. Was he eager to hear the scoop or was he in a hurry?

"It was good."

"Did you learn anything?"

"Yes, I learned how to do the buffalo."

"No," he said, apparently unaware that she'd been joking, "did you learn anything about the *case*?"

"Bob, it was only my first class. I thought I was supposed to be undercover. Did you want me to be obvious about it?" Although she was now wondering if obvious was the way to go. It seemed to be working for Gertrude. "Besides,

I couldn't get a word in edgewise with Gertrude around."

Bob didn't say anything, so Sandra sneaked a peek at him. "Do you know her?"

He rubbed his hands together. "I do not. But I've heard stories."

She waited for more. "What kind of stories?"

"She fancies herself a private investigator."

Sandra snickered. She couldn't imagine it.

"You laugh, but she's not terrible at it. She's actually managed to put a few things together. Remember that murder at Gunslinger City?"

"Just barely, but she did mention that tonight."

He raised an eyebrow. "Seriously? Did she give you all a rundown of her resume?"

Sandra nodded as she slowed down to turn onto another road. "Sort of."

"I popped in for a few minutes to check on you, but I couldn't stay. Did I miss anything?"

Sandra shook her head. "Not really."

"You didn't see anything interesting?"

"Not really."

"Or unusual?" He was starting to sound frustrated.

She didn't want to frustrate an angel. She tried to think harder. What had she seen that was odd? "There's a woman in the class,

Mandi. She's a bit suspicious. Though she could just be shy and socially awkward. I'm not sure that makes her a murderer."

"Uh-huh. What else?"

Her grip on the wheel tightened. Then she thought of something that made her smile. "Well, I thought it was a little odd that Gertrude had a perfectly normal-looking older gentleman waiting for her in the parking lot."

"Really?" He sounded intrigued.

Good. She'd finally managed to intrigue him.

"Yes, really. And he was in a really nice vehicle. A big, shiny, black four-door pickup. Looked brand-new." She caught herself feeling a bit covetous. She couldn't imagine driving a new vehicle. She glanced down at her odometer and winced: 232,440 miles on frost-heaved and pot-holed roads.

"Maybe he's her husband?"

Sandra almost snorted. "Maybe. But I'm telling you. He looked normal. Respectable." She hadn't checked, but she was willing to bet he'd even been wearing two socks.

"Anything else?"

Shoot. He was done being intrigued. But there was something else, wasn't there? Oh yes, she'd almost forgotten. "There was another man in the parking lot. I thought it was strange because I hung around till everyone left, trying to talk to Joyelle, but Gertrude was hogging her, so I finally left because it was so obvious that I was lurking. Anyway, I followed Mandi out, and she got into her car. So, the only people left in the building were Joyelle and Gertrude. Yet there was another man waiting in a car."

"Maybe he was waiting for Joyelle."

"I don't think so. She had a car there, and he drove away before either of them came out. In fact, he drove away as soon as I stared at him … as soon as Mandi left, actually." She shuddered remembering the man. "He gave my sixth sense the shivers."

"Why?"

"I'm not sure. He was wearing dark sunglasses—at night. But it was more than that … I don't know."

"Mama, I'm hungry."

They'd just driven by McDonald's. "I know, honey, we're almost home."

"Really?" He dragged the word out to make it last three syllables.

"Really."

"So maybe he was following Mandi."

"Maybe? I don't know."

And then Bob was gone. She hated it when he did that. She'd thought that they were in the middle of a conversation and then poof! No more Bob.

Chapter 19

Joyelle called Sandra on Thursday morning. She had just dropped the kids off at school and was wrestling a sticky Sammy out of his car seat. His sister had given him one of her Pop-Tarts while they were en route, and Sandra wished she hadn't. Still, even though her fingers were covered in Wildlicious Wild Berry goo, she grabbed for the phone when she saw who was calling, letting Sammy plop back into his seat.

Despite her excitement, she hesitated before answering. Why was Joyelle calling *her*? Was something wrong? Had Joyelle figured out that Sandra was really a fraud and that she had no intention of dancing in the recital? Sammy managed to climb out on his own and wrapped his sticky arms around her neck. She swiped to answer the phone and then turned to head into the house, leaving the van door open behind her.

If a thief decided to target the Provost family, he or she would soon regret it.

"Hello?" Her voice came out a bit froggy, thanks to Sammy's small but mighty bicep.

"Good morning," Joyelle sang. "Are you okay?"

"Yes, sorry." She adjusted Sammy's weight to take some of the pressure off her larynx. "Just trying to get the baby inside. What's up?" She tried to use the hand holding Sammy to open her front door, and she started to lose him. "Hang on," she said, embarrassed at how breathless she sounded. She put her son down, and he started to scream, still holding onto her neck, so she stayed bent over as she unlocked the door. When it swung open, she tried to stand up, but he wasn't going to let her do that without him. "Let go," she said gently.

He did nothing of the sort.

"Let go, Sammy," she tried again.

Nothing.

"Let go!" she snapped, and he let go so that he could put both hands to his face and wail like a banshee. "Go inside, Sammy!" She wasn't trying to holler at him, but she raised her voice to be heard over his wails and then was horrified, imagining how she must sound to Joyelle. She gently herded the child inside, and Mr. T squirted out by his legs. Mr. T wasn't an outside cat, but she would deal with that later. She ran to get Sammy's toy tablet, turned it on, and shoved it into his sticky hands.

He immediately quit crying.

"So sorry, Joyelle," she said, collapsing on the couch.

"Don't be. I had children, don't forget. I can call back at another time if that would be helpful?"

"No, it's okay now. He's happy." And filthy. And the cat's gone. "What's up?"

"Well ..." She sounded nervous. "I was wondering, and it's okay if you're too busy, but I was wondering if we could have lunch. I wanted to talk to you about some stuff, and ... it's my treat. Anywhere you want."

Sandra opened her mouth to accept the invitation, but Joyelle kept talking. "Although maybe the McDonald's playground is the best bet."

Sandra laughed at the absurdity of that idea. Sammy was way too little to keep himself safely occupied in the McDonald's play area. He'd be ecstatic, but then he'd get stuck in a corner or a net, and she'd have to crawl in to rescue him. She'd learned that lesson with her first child. Never let them loose in a McDonald's playground until they were old enough to rescue themselves.

"How about the Italian place on Factory Street, and you don't have to buy my lunch." If she was going to actually go to a restaurant, she wanted it to be a good one, and she loved The Elbow Room.

"I love The Elbow Room!" Joyelle sang. "But it's pretty fancy for a toddler?"

"Oh, don't worry, he won't be coming along. I have a dear friend who loves to babysit."

"Oh, how perfect. All right then, twelve o'clock?"

She didn't want to wait that long. The suspense would kill her. "Can you go any earlier?" Like maybe nine o'clock? That was a perfectly reasonable time for pasta, wasn't it?

"I think they open at eleven. Will that work?"

"Absolutely." She hesitated. "Is everything okay?"

"Oh yes. Nothing to worry about. I could just use a friend."

"Okay great," Sandra said too quickly. "I can be a friend." Her cheeks grew warm. How much of a dork was she?

Joyelle laughed. "Perfect! I'll see you then!"

Sandra hung up the phone and looked at Sammy. He'd spread his Wildlicious goodness to the tablet. She stood up, grabbed him, and went outside. She would deal with the Wildlicious later. First, they had to find Mr. T.

Chapter 20

"Mr. T!" Sandra called. "Mr. T!" She knew she probably wasn't calling loudly enough, but really, what were the chances the cat was going to come? And Sandra was deeply embarrassed by her cat's name. What if one of her neighbors saw that the cat was female and then heard Sandra calling her Mr. T? They'd think she was an imbecile. An imbecile who was a big fan of *The A-Team*. She was neither. She didn't even think she'd been alive when *The A-Team* had aired, but her beloved husband loved his TV Land, and they'd been marathoning Hannibal and crew when they'd adopted Mr. T. The poor cat. She'd grown up listening to things blow up. To this day, she was rarely startled. Remembering this made Sandra's heart swell for the sweet kitty, and she called out to her with more volume.

Still, she saw no signs of her and decided she'd best go home to get a can of tuna. She turned back, and Sammy banged his fake tablet on the stroller tray. "Careful, honey. That will break, and then you won't have it anymore."

When she looked up, she saw a car coming toward them at a remarkably slow speed. It took her a second to recognize it, but when she did, her heart raced. It was the creepy man from the dance parking lot. She pretended she didn't recognize him and resisted the urge to sprint home. Maybe it was a coincidence that he was on her street going two miles per hour. She picked up her speed a little. Sammy started to sing. She continued to call for Mr. T.

She heard the car turn around and come their way.

If she hadn't had Sammy, she might have continued to feign innocence, but she *did* have Sammy, so she took off at a sprint, pushing the stroller in front of her. Sammy cackled in delight and threw both hands up into the wind. The fake tablet tumbled to the sidewalk, but Sandra didn't slow down. She could come back for that later. No one was going to pick up a Wildlicious-caked fake tablet off the sidewalk.

She turned to go up the walk, and she heard the car slow. "Bob!" she cried aloud. "Where are you?" She didn't pause to take Sammy out of the stroller. She just turned and dragged the thing backward up her front steps. Sammy cackled in delight. He was having a great time. Because she was now facing the street, she could see the car and the driver.

His face was turned toward her, but he didn't stop. Instead, he accelerated and disappeared.

She looked at the license plate: TFS6FL.

No way was she going to remember that. Her brain spun. *Toby Flenderson snorted 6 fruit loops.* There. She'd remember *that*.

She sat down on her porch swing and tried to gather herself.

"Don't look at me," Bob said.

She looked.

He was sitting beside her. "Some of your neighbors are watching you. Don't say anything. Maybe we should go inside."

She didn't want to go inside. She wanted to sit right where she was until her limbs stopped shaking. "Do you know where my cat is?" she cried.

He frowned. "Your cat?"

"Yes, my cat. And where *were* you?"

"I came as soon as you called!" He sounded defensive.

She made a mental note to call him sooner next time. She looked at the street, and a curtain across the road fell shut. "Who *was* that guy?"

"I don't know. Want me to follow him?"

"Yes!" she cried, and he vanished.

She took her cell phone out of the stroller's cup holder. When she looked down at it, she realized she hadn't needed her fancy mnemonic. She could've just typed the license plate number into the phone. She laughed at herself, and Sammy laughed too. She looked at his big smile. "You're a pretty good partner, Sammo." She called Chip.

He answered on the first ring.

This made her smile. "Hi, Chip. Sandra Provost. Yesterday, after dance class, I saw a man sitting alone in the parking lot, and that same man just chased me in his car." She wasn't sure he'd actually *chased* her, but she didn't want to give Chip any reason not to be alarmed.

"I'll be right there." He sounded appropriately wary.

"I'm not sure you have to come. I got the plate number."

"Good job!" He sounded genuinely proud of her.

She closed her eyes and pictured the mnemonic device so she could share only the pertinent letters. "T ... F ... S ... 6 ... F ... L." That was it, right? Toby Flenderson hadn't snorted five fruit loops? Or seven?

"Is that it?"

"Yep."

"Are you sure?"

"Yes, why?"

"You just recited that back awfully slowly, as if you were having trouble remembering."

No, she had no trouble remembering, thanks to her little trick; she was just having trouble *relaying* it without also relaying said trick. "That's the number. I'd bet the farm on it."

He laughed. "All right. We'll run the plates. I'll be right there."

She sat there a bit dazed. What should she do now? She still needed to find Mr. T, but was it safe? And who knew what was going to happen when Bob returned with his report? *If* he returned. Her arms still shaking, she unsnapped Sammy from the stroller and carried him inside. She plopped him in the sink, hosed him off, and then she called Ethel.

Chapter 21

Sandra pulled into her driveway to find Bob sitting on her porch swing. "Where have you been?" he cried when she climbed out of the van.

She chuckled at the role reversal. "I ran Sammy over to Ethel's."

"Oh," he said, his frustration softening. "She must have been happy about that."

"Yes." She slammed her minivan door. "So was he. I think he likes her better than me anyway."

"Not true," Bob said. "And remember, your neighbors can hear you. Maybe we should go inside." He started to get up, but she motioned to him to stay sitting.

She sat beside him, and the swing rocked forward. "Nah, I like it out here, and the neighbors already think I'm crazy. Besides, Chip is on his way. In fact, I'm surprised he's not here already." It had taken her at least twenty minutes to get Sammy deposited.

"He's been here. He left."

She looked at Bob. "Really?"

"Yep, he came to the door, said a naughty word when you didn't answer, and then left."

She snickered. "A naughty word?"

"Yes." He didn't understand why she found this amusing.

"And you just sat there watching?"

"What did you want me to do? Hog-tie him till you got back?"

"No," she said thoughtfully. She didn't know what she wished he'd done. She just found it amusing that he'd sat there and secretly stared at the detective.

"How often do angels do that?"

"Do what?"

"How often do angels secretly watch us humans doing our thing?"

"Well, we watch you all the time, but that isn't much of a secret."

She would've asked him to expound on that, but a black SUV pulled into her driveway. She hoped it would only contain Chip, but nope, Slaughter climbed out too.

Sandra groaned.

"Be kind," Bob said.

"Where'd you go?" Chip said accusingly, and then didn't give her a chance to answer. "I called you!"

Oops. She'd left her phone in the van when she'd gone into Ethel's. It was still there now. "Sorry. I took my youngest to Ethel's. Figured he'd be safer there."

Robin Merrill

Slaughter glared at her. Sandra refused to give her the satisfaction of meeting her gaze, but she could still feel the heat. They came up the walk, and Sandra tried to be patient.

"Did you run the plate?" she asked when Chip got close enough that she could.

He gave her a wry smile. "Listen to you with all your cop talk." He stopped and rested his foot on her bottom step and leaned on his knee. "We have him in custody."

"Already?"

"Don't sound so surprised," Slaughter said slowly.

"I'm not surprised ..." Sandra didn't know how to win with this woman. "I'm just impressed."

"Well, don't be," Chip said. "He went straight home from here."

"Did he say why he was following me?"

A creepy smile spread across Slaughter's face. Sandra didn't know what it meant.

"Yes," Chip said, wearing a small smile of his own. "He said he was trying to figure out who killed Jazmyn Jecks."

Bob groaned, and it took all of Sandra's willpower not to look at him.

"And he thinks I did it?" Sandra cried, indignant.

107

"He thinks," Chip said, "that it was someone from the dance studio because that's where she died—"

"Buker!" Slaughter interrupted. "This is an ongoing investigation. She's not a cop."

Chip slid his eyes toward her. "No, she's not, but I like to catch murderers, and she's good at that. I'm not asking her to go after the guy. I'm just letting her use her brain, which happens to be good with this stuff."

Sandra tried not to beam with pride.

"Anyway …" Chip turned his attention back to Sandra. "He said he thinks it's the owner …" Chip flipped through his mental notes. "Joyelle Blaine."

"*Pfft!* It wasn't Joyelle," Sandra said.

"What makes you say that?" Chip asked.

"I just know. Trust me. So, if he suspects her, why was he following me?"

Chip raised an eyebrow. "Apparently you're supposed to have lunch with her today?"

Sandra scowled. "How does he know that?"

"Says he overheard her talking on the phone."

"That's creepy."

Chip shrugged. "Maybe. Depends on where she was when she was talking on the phone."

"And if she was in her kitchen?"

"Well, then, yes, that would be creepy. He gave us his version of events. Can you give me a detailed account of what happened?"

Sandra told him, leaving nothing out, not even the Wildlicious Pop-Tart, which got an eye roll from Slaughter.

"He didn't break any laws, I'm afraid. If it continues, you'll be able to get a restraining order on him, but I doubt it will happen again." Chip looked around her yard, up at her roof, and then at the sky. It was a bizarre scan of his surroundings, and Sandra couldn't quite interpret it. "You call me if *anything* happens, but ... are you going to be okay? I'm thinking maybe you shouldn't be alone." His eyes darted around her yard again, and she could have sworn he looked right at Bob, as if he was *trying* to see who was sitting beside her.

"I'll be fine. If I'm not, I'll call you." She was touched by his concern.

He nodded, his jaw set. "Okay. Glad you're all right. Hope you find your cat." He turned to go, and Slaughter, after one final dirty look at Sandra, followed.

When they were gone, Bob groaned again. "This is not good."

"What?"

"Why does everyone think they are a detective all of a sudden? First Gertrude and now this guy? We do not need three different amateurs muddling around in this case."

"Four," Sandra said without looking at him.

"Four what?"

"Four amateurs." She looked at him.

"Are you serious? Who else? Who's the fourth?"

"You are, silly."

Chapter 22

The Elbow Room's parking lot was empty except for Joyelle's car. This was a good thing as the lot was problematically small. The restaurant had given a second life to an old abandoned shoe factory. Sandra had always wondered where all those workers had parked. Had they all walked to work back them?

As she walked to the door, she realized her excitement was unreasonable. Why was she so hyped up? Because she had a new friend? She really did like Joyelle. It would be very cool to be her friend. Or was she excited to get the scoop? Or was it simply the garlic bread?

The hostess smiled and welcomed her, and Sandra explained she was meeting someone.

"Right this way." She led her to a cozy table in the corner, where Joyelle was stabbing at her phone screen.

"Everything okay?" Sandra said, sensing her frustration.

"Oh yes." She smiled brightly and put her phone down. "I was just killing some zombies while I waited."

"Oh."

The hostess laid a menu atop the cloth napkin in front of her and left.

"Thanks for meeting me." Joyelle folded her hands in front of her. "I'll let you spend some time with the menu before I bend your ear."

"That's all right. I already know what I want."

"Really? I'm impressed. Takes me forever to make decisions like that. I'm always afraid I'll miss something." She tittered.

"So, what's going on?"

"Well, I don't really know how to ask this, so I'm just going to come right out with it." She took a big breath. "I know that you're only taking the adult class so you can figure out who killed Jazmyn." She leaned back a little. "At least, I *think* that."

Sandra didn't know what to say, so she said nothing. How had Joyelle figured her out so easily? If she hadn't had such success going undercover on the soccer field, she would think she was an undercover fail. Of course, that success *had* gotten her shoved into a trunk and flung off a cliff, so maybe *success* wasn't the right word. She let out a long breath. "Something like that, yes." She hurried to add, "But I do enjoy the class and am grateful for the opportunity."

Joyelle nodded quickly as if she didn't believe a word Sandra was saying. "The thing is ..." She looked around furtively and then leaned in closer. "I've never been this close to a murder investigation before, and I had no idea it would be like this."

When she didn't elaborate, Sandra said, "Like what?"

Joyelle's eyes widened a little, and Sandra realized she was wearing fake eyelashes. "Like all these people coming out of the woodwork to try to solve the case! I didn't know there were so many Miss Marples in the world!"

That was the second time someone had called Sandra Miss Marple. She tried not to be offended.

Joyelle held up a hand. "Not calling *you* Miss Marple, sorry. But there's this crazy Gertrude woman. Who *is* she? And then now there's Ivan Clark, who's even crazier than Gertrude—"

"Who?"

Joyelle's eyes fell shut, and she took a deep breath. "Ivan Clark is a local man, and one of the weirdest people on the planet. He was obsessed with Jazmyn. I don't know much about him other than he's creepy and he hangs around the studio all the time, and he's at all our events. He followed us to

Washington D.C. for a competition. Can you believe that? I couldn't!"

Was this the same guy who'd followed her? "Does he drive a beat-up cream-colored car and wear dark glasses?"

Joyelle nodded emphatically. "Yes! Do you know him?"

"No, but I saw him on Tuesday when I came out of the studio. He left after Mandi did. I wondered if he was following her—"

"Oh, so do you know Mandi?"

"No, I heard her introduce herself to Gertrude."

Joyelle winced.

"Anyway, then this morning, he was following me down my street." Sandra told her the whole story, finishing with the statement that Ivan Clark was now in police custody, though, admittedly, probably not for long.

"Maybe a little jail time will smarten him up. Did you find your cat?"

Sandra smiled. "I did. She came home on her own while I was out looking for her. She was sitting on the porch looking annoyed that no one was home to let her in."

Joyelle chuckled knowingly. "That sounds about right. Anyway, I really want this whole thing to be over. Jazmyn was a pain in my backside the whole time I knew her, and now that she's gone, she's even more of a pain. I've got three hobby detectives interfering with my life." She paused. "No offense."

"None taken." *And there's four*, Sandra thought. Hadn't Joyelle prayed for help? And God had sent a slew of it!

"If I'm going to have my life disturbed, I'd like the duration of this disturbing to be as short as possible. You are, by far, the least offensive of the hobby sleuths, so I'd love to help you figure this thing out."

Uh-oh. Bob wasn't going to like this. There was such a thing as too many cooks in the kitchen. There was probably also such a thing as too many snoops in the murder mystery.

"I don't mean I'm going to chase anyone around or carry a gun or anything," Joyelle clarified. "But I thought maybe if we put our heads together, this could all be over sooner."

Sandra nodded. "Sure. That makes sense."

The server returned to take their orders, and both women conveyed their requests quickly, eager to get back to the task at hand.

Joyelle held her arms out to her sides. "So, what do you want to know? I don't know much about Jazmyn, but I'll tell you anything and everything I can."

"Was she from around here?"

Joyelle nodded. "She said she grew up up north. Why do you ask?"

Sandra shrugged and took a sip of her water. "Not sure. She just didn't look like she was from around here."

"That is true."

Sandra couldn't think of anything else to ask about Jazmyn. "Did you know that Ivan knew about this lunch of ours?"

Joyelle looked horrified. "What?"

"Yes, he told the police that he overheard you talking on the phone with me."

Her horror visibly grew.

"Do you remember where you were when you were talking to me?"

She nodded, and her face had grown paler. "I was in my backyard, sitting in a lawn chair watching the birds."

Yikes. "Anywhere in your backyard a creepy hobby detective could have hidden?"

She nodded again. "Lots of places. Guess I'll make my calls from inside the house from now on."

Chapter 23

Joyelle winked at Sandra when she walked into the studio to drop Joanna off. She and Sandra had been in constant contact since their lunch, but Sandra still hadn't learned anything pertinent to the case. By all accounts, Jazmyn Jecks had been a selfish, despicable woman, and no one missed her. Yet, Joyelle couldn't think of anyone who cared enough about her to kill her.

It had happened in the dance studio. Therefore, Sandra was confident that Jazmyn's death had something to do with dance.

Joyelle respectfully, wholeheartedly disagreed. Wishful thinking, maybe?

Joanna's class ended with great jubilee, and she came running out of the studio to show her mother her new moves. Sandra slid her paperback into her purse and bent to lace up her new tap shoes while she watched her daughter cut a rug. She stood, patted her on the head, and said, "Good job, honey. You're going to have to tutor me."

Joanna beamed with the praise, and Sandra left her to clap-clap her way into the studio. She hadn't exaggerated. Joanna was picking this all up much faster than her mother was.

Class started, and Gertrude was nowhere to be seen. Sandra was a bit disappointed at this. Gertrude was entertaining, and her brazen questioning offered Sandra more fodder to analyze. She wasn't finding much fodder on her own. But Gertrude wasn't there, and Sandra knew that Joyelle was relieved. Maybe she had given up. Maybe she wouldn't be back.

The classes flew by, and Sandra enjoyed trying to keep up. She was grateful she planned to quit before doing this in front of any crowd bigger than the one she was already in.

She and Joanna waited until everyone else had left before leaving Joyelle alone to lock up. When they stepped out into the cool night, Sandra spotted that same ugly cream-colored car. It was parked on the other side of the small parking lot, facing her. She wanted to go pound on the window and ask him what he was doing, but she had Joanna with her, so instead, she hustled her daughter into the safety of the minivan and then climbed behind the wheel.

"That man is here again," Bob said.

Sandra jumped. "Will you *please* stop doing that? It's not good for me to be so startled so often."

"I would think you would get used to it."

"Hi, Bob," Joanna chirped.

"Hi, cutie pie."

"His name is Ivan Clark," Sandra said.

"I thought the police told him to stop interfering."

Sandra laughed and looked at him in wonder. "How many times have they told us the same thing?"

Bob raised his eyebrows. "The police have never told *me* anything."

She rolled her eyes and turned the key.

"You should go ask him what he's doing here."

She stared at him, surprised. She'd had the same idea, but now that the angel in the front seat was suggesting it, she was annoyed. "I know what he's doing here. He's snooping."

"He should have joined the adult dance class with you and Gertrude."

"Was that a joke? Did the angel just make a joke?"

He smiled, but it looked fake. "I feel there's more to it."

"You feel? Are you using some sort of angel sense?"

"Sort of."

She hesitated, the car still in park.

"Go ahead. I'll stay with Joanna. If anything goes wrong, I'll be right there."

She did sort of want to go confront the guy. If he was rude or scary, she'd soon regret it, but she wanted to get a closer look at the man who had chased her down her street. She got out of the van and tried to appear strong and resolute as she strode across the pavement. Though he watched her come, he did not roll down the window to greet her, so she rapped on it with her knuckles.

Still, he didn't roll it down.

She put her hands on her hips. "Do you want me to holler my questions?" she said as loudly as she could.

He cranked his window down. The old-fashioned way. This was an old car. "What?"

"Hi, I'm Sandra. What are you doing?"

"None of your business." He was trying to sound tough, but he obviously wasn't. Creepy still, but not tough.

"It is my business when you chase me and my son down the street, and now you're sitting here in the dark watching me."

"I explained that to the cops, and I'm not watching you."

"Then what are you doing?"

"I'm waiting for Joyelle to come out."

"So you're watching her?"

"Did you ever think I might be trying to *protect* her?" He raised a patronizing eyebrow.

She almost snorted. She thought Joyelle would stand a better chance on her own. "Joyelle doesn't want you here. She can take care of herself." Sandra noticed that his car was jam-packed full of stuff. Boxes and bags of random stuff: folders full of paper, picture frames, lots of clothes. "Are you moving?"

"How do you know she doesn't want me here?"

"She told me. Are you moving?" she asked again.

Ivan suddenly panicked and rolled up the window as fast as his slim arm would let him and then started his car, which took two tries. Then he peeled out of the parking lot, almost running over her toes.

What a strange man, she thought.

She returned to her minivan and the waiting supernatural being.

"Well?" Bob asked once she was safely ensconced in the minivan again.

"Well what?" She put the van in reverse.

"What did you learn?"

She put her foot on the brake and looked at her friend. "I didn't learn anything, but there was something strange. He had a bunch of clothes in his car."

"Clothes? Maybe he had to do laundry."

"They were shiny. I saw glitter. And lots of pink."

"Maybe he wears women's clothes."

"Or maybe he had someone else's clothes in his car."

"Oh," Bob said slowly. "That *is* creepy." He looked behind the van. "Let's get Joanna home." He now spoke like a man with a plan.

"And then what?"

"Then we go see if any of Jazmyn's clothes are missing."

Chapter 24

Sandra stood looking up at the apartment building. "How are we going to get in?" Every apartment opened to the outside, so they only had to get through one door, but they had to do it without the neighbors knowing, and as far as she knew, Bob didn't have a plan for that.

A black cat meowed from the balcony. Sandra hoped he or she hadn't been Jazmyn's cat. It wasn't wearing a sparkly collar, so probably not.

"I'll take care of it."

Surprised, Sandra followed him up the stairs to the second-floor apartment. Was he really going to use his power for breaking and entering? Hadn't he refused to do that in the past? She couldn't recall a specific incident, but she was sure it had happened at some point.

When he reached the door, it swung open. Did that count as breaking and entering? He hadn't even touched it. "Shh," he said and stepped inside. She followed him into the darkness and closed the door behind her. The place smelled like fruit shampoo. Apple, she thought.

Bob handed her a flashlight.

"Thanks. Don't you need it?"

"I can see."

She turned on the flashlight and saw they were in a kitchen. An extraordinarily messy kitchen. As she looked around, she realized it was messy in more ways than one. Had Jazmyn been a slob? Or had a slob been squatting there since she died? Or maybe someone had ransacked the place. If so, they hadn't flipped furniture over or cut up sofa cushions, but several drawers and cupboards were open. She noticed something and quickly darted around the apartment to confirm her observation's validity before sharing.

Just as she'd thought. "Bob," she whispered. "There are no photographs."

"What?" He came to stand beside her and looked around for himself. "You're right." He looked at her. "I'm not sure that means anything. Some people aren't into photos. Maybe she hadn't lived here long."

"Look at all this stuff. She's been here awhile. And Bob, that woman was *vain*. If she didn't have pictures of herself, I'll eat my hat."

"So, what are you saying?"

"I saw picture frames in Ivan's car."

"Really?" Now he was interested. He looked around again. "That is weird."

"I thought so. I'm going to go look at her clothes." She took a few steps toward a closed door on the other side of the small living room. "If he left any behind, that is."

In the bedroom, the smell of apple shampoo intensified. As she'd expected, the dresser drawers stood open, and it appeared they'd been rifled through. If he'd taken her clothes, and Sandra was certain that he had, he hadn't taken all of them.

Dust marks on her nightstand suggested he'd also taken a picture frame from this room. He hadn't taken all the frames in the house, though. On the wall to her left hung a large frame that displayed what Sandra assumed to be a high school cheerleading uniform. She would have laughed if she weren't so stunned.

Bob came up behind her and whistled. "There's something wrong with this man."

"Indeed." She shone her flashlight at the uniform. "I think there was something wrong with Jazmyn too."

He scowled. "There's nothing wrong with being proud of your athletic accomplishments."

Sandra scowled back. "It's a *cheerleading* uniform!"

"Have you *seen* what cheerleaders do?" he scolded. "They are strong, flexible gymnasts!"

"Fine, whatever," she mumbled. God had put this being in charge of sports. She probably shouldn't argue with him in his area of expertise.

He was still staring at the uniform.

"What are you thinking?"

He shook his head. "I don't recognize it."

"Well, Jazmyn wasn't a kid anymore. That uniform is probably fairly old."

He was still shaking his head. "No, I would still recognize it. I've been doing this for a while now, and this isn't from around here. It looks like a high school uniform, but high school or junior high, purple and yellow are not common school colors. I can think of a few, but their mascots are cats."

"Cats?"

"Yes, various felines. Panthers, wildcats, lions, etc."

Sandra watched him stare at the uniform. She certainly hoped it was from high school. That was weird enough. Framing and hanging a junior high uniform would be next level bizarre. "So, she's from away." Was this development really that significant?

Bob pulled his eyes away from the uniform and looked at Sandra. "That mascot is probably a mustang," he said thoughtfully.

"We've only got one mustangs school here, and they are green and gold." He looked back at the uniform. "Or maybe that's a charger."

Sandra followed his gaze. "Maybe it's just a horse."

"Nobody has *horses* for a mascot." His level of disgust alarmed her.

"I was kidding."

He wasn't amused. "There are purple and gold chargers in Michigan, but that's a tiny Christian school."

"Michigan? Just how much random sports information do you know?"

He looked at her. "Would you like to know the stats for the 1636 Algonquian stick ball championship?"

"You're kidding."

He returned his eyes to the uniform. "I am not." He stared quietly for a minute. "There is a mustangs school in Arkansas, also a Christian school."

What was it with Christians and their horses?

"That one's a bit larger. And there's another one in California, but they opened only a few years ago." He scratched his jaw. "Oh, and there's one in Texas ... and one in Illinois." He smacked himself on the forehead and then looked at her wide-eyed. "It could be a bronco. I didn't think of that." He sounded so disappointed in himself.

"It's okay, Bob. I'm not sure we need to know where it's from."

"And it could be from a college," he said as if he hadn't heard her.

"I don't think Jazmyn went to college."

His eyes snapped toward hers. "Now you're just being catty."

"Maybe. Sorry. Maybe we should go break into Ivan's place." She shone her flashlight around the room. "See what he took from here."

Bob laughed. "Weren't you against breaking into *this* one? And that's considerably more dangerous. He's a lunatic."

"Well, we wouldn't do it while he was *there*."

"I am not sure that would tell us much. If he took a single item, then sure, that would probably be a clue as to his motive. But when he takes many things? That means less. That only means he is crazy." He looked contemplative. "I'm not saying that it's out of the question. But you should first make sure that Chip knows that Ivan broke into this place."

Sandra sighed. "Yes, that is a good idea. But let's finish looking around first." It didn't take long to explore Jazmyn's bedroom. There was nothing of note under the bed, only some spare blankets. Her nightstand drawer held nothing exciting. She shone her flashlight into the small closet—a tremendous crash sounded from the other side of the apartment.

Bob disappeared.

Chapter 25

Like the limited human being that she was, Sandra used her feet to rush toward the noise. She wished she could teleport like Bob, but wishes weren't horses. If they were, they'd probably be a mascot for some Christian school.

A man's voice whispered, "I *told* you to step on the chair." Flashlights flickered through the doorway.

"I *did* step on the chair!" a croaky voice said with no attempt to be quiet. "But it moved!"

It took Sandra a few seconds to place the voice. She stepped into the opening. "Gertrude?"

Gertrude screamed.

"Quiet!" Sandra and Gertrude's male friend said in unison.

Gertrude rubbed her hip. "I think I hurt myself."

"Well, you did just fall through a window," the man said.

"Not for the first time." Gertrude sounded proud of how many times she'd fallen through a window. "Where's my walker?"

"Right here." Her sidekick slid it over to her.

"Thank you," she said and then looked at Sandra. "What are you doing? Don't you know it's illegal to break into a crime scene?"

"Would you please keep your voice down?" Sandra whispered. She looked behind Gertrude at the window they'd just come through. It must have been a tight squeeze. She went and looked out the window to see a rickety fire escape stretching to the ground. "Why didn't you just use the front door?"

"Because we *didn't have a key*," Gertrude said as if Sandra were the stupidest person alive.

Sandra shone her flashlight at the man's chest. She wanted to get a good look at him without blinding him. Yes, it was the man from the parking lot.

"Who are you?" he asked.

"I'm Sandra," she whispered.

"What are you doing here?" Though the man was illegally standing in an apple shampoo-scented apartment, his slacks and shirt were pressed, and his sparse hair was combed into place. She could easily imagine him in a study with elbow patches and a pipe.

"I could ask you two the same thing. At least I *knew* Jazmyn." This was only sort of a lie. A half-lie, maybe. A baby lie.

"Don't lie to me," Gertrude said matter-of-factly and headed into the apartment.

The man stared at Sandra as if waiting for her to go next.

She followed Gertrude into the hallway, wondering where Bob was hiding. She didn't want to accidentally step on his toes.

"This place is a mess!" Gertrude said looking around. "Very unorganized." She went into the bedroom.

Sandra went back into the living room. Jazmyn hadn't had a lot of books on her bookshelf, but those that were there looked undisturbed. She went in for a closer look. Sure enough, there were no streaks in the dust. She studied the bindings of the books. A spattering of bestsellers from over the years and a history book about Mount Green, Michigan. Sandra pulled the slim volume from its spot and flipped it over to scan the back cover by flashlight.

The History of Mount Green told the story, mostly in sepia photographs, of the birth and growth of the small Midwestern town of Mount Green.

Yearbook, she thought. A woman who kept her high school cheerleading uniform in a glass case would definitely have kept her yearbooks.

"Well, that's mighty peculiar," Gertrude said through the wall.

She'd probably noticed the uniform.

There were no yearbooks on the shelf. This was disappointing. Still, she clutched the Mount Green book in her hand. That was too unusual to not mean something. She wanted to talk it over with Bob, but she'd have to wait. She went to the kitchen and rummaged around. Jazmyn didn't have a lot of cooking utensils. She did have a stack of bills, and many of the envelopes featured big red letters. Jazmyn owed some people some money. The electric company. Several credit cards. Her satellite television provider. But she'd likely not been too worried about any of this because the envelopes remained unopened.

Sandra opened one of the credit card bills. Might as well see what Jazmyn had been buying. She gasped when she saw the balance. Why would they give this woman such a high credit line? She scanned the list of charges: restaurants, clothing stores, an upscale spa and salon, the Coach online store, and bars. Lots of bars.

Sandra opened the fridge door to find a few six-packs of craft beer, some condiments, and two half-gallons of organic soy milk.

"Hungry?" Gertrude asked from behind, making Sandra jump.

She stood up so fast she rapped her head on the bottom of the freezer. She winced but did her best to keep her pain to herself. "No," she said, trying not to whimper. She shut the fridge door.

"What's that in your hand?"

Sandra looked down. "Oh, nothing. Just a book." She slowly brought her eyes up to meet Gertrude's. She *really* didn't want to share her theory with this woman.

"What kind of a book?" Gertrude stepped closer.

Sandra didn't know what to say. "A history book," she said lamely.

"What kind of history book?" Gertrude stepped still closer.

Sandra wanted to back up, but there was a refrigerator in her way. She held the book up so Gertrude could see it, but she kept a death grip on it.

Gertrude leaned over her walker and peered at the cover. "Mount Green." She looked at Sandra. "You sure are attached to that book."

"Yes, ma'am," she said because she didn't know what else to say.

Gertrude grunted and recoiled. "Don't call me ma'am."

Chapter 26

Blue lights flashed through the windows.

Gertrude's male friend swore.

"Watch your mouth!" Gertrude said. "It's no bother. I'll just explain that I'm a P.I."

"You're not a P.I.," the man said. He went to the window and looked out. "Not even close. And this looks like State Troopers."

Sandra's stomach rolled. Best to meet this thing head-on. She ripped open the door with one hand raised.

"What are you doing?" Gertrude grabbed for her, but it was too late.

Car doors slammed. There was one cruiser and one SUV.

"I *told you* it would be her." Slaughter's voice drifted up through the darkness.

"And I didn't argue," Chip said. "Did you find anything?" he called up.

"Sort of."

"You did?" Gertrude said from behind her. She didn't sound happy.

Chip was on his way up the stairs. He frowned. "Is someone else in there?"

"Sort of?" She didn't want to lie to Chip, but she didn't want to be a rat either.

Chip's hand went toward his hip.

"No, no," Sandra said. "It's only Gertrude."

"Tattle-tale," Gertrude mumbled.

Chip's hand fell away.

"Gertrude and her chauffeur."

Chip stepped inside and felt along the wall for a light switch. "Might as well throw some light on the subject." His fingers found what they were searching for, and the kitchen exploded with light. Sandra squinted and shut her flashlight off. Bob stood across the room leaning against the wall.

Chip looked around, one hand on his hip. "My, my, what do we have here? An amateur sleuth convention?"

"That is what happens when you don't *throw them in jail*," Slaughter said, stepping into the apartment.

Chip looked at Gertrude. "You're trespassing."

"What about her?" Gertrude cried, pointing.

"She has my permission to be here."

"She does?" Gertrude cried, incredulous.

I do? Sandra wondered.

Chip took out his notepad and asked for Gertrude and company's names and addresses. They answered willingly enough, and Sandra learned that the chauffeur's name was Calvin. It seemed to suit him. Chip stopped writing and looked at them. "Did you two find anything helpful?"

"If we did," Gertrude said slowly, "why would we tell you?"

Chip's face twisted into a scowl. Slaughter put her head in her hand and rubbed at her temples.

"Because we're *the police*," Chip said.

"I'm sorry, Detective," the chauffeur named Calvin said. "Sometimes Gertrude doesn't think before she speaks." He glared down at her and then gave his attention back to Chip. "She just really wants to solve this case herself."

"Why?" Chip asked.

"Why?" Calvin repeated, as if he didn't quite understand the question. "I'm not sure why. This is just what she does."

"I want the credit," Gertrude said. "For my resume. I'm moving to South Dakota soon, and I am going to open a private investigating business."

"South Dakota?" Chip said. "Why?"

"She's not moving anywhere," Calvin said and glared at her again. "We didn't find anything. If it's all right with you, we'll be on our way."

Chip didn't answer him at first. Then he motioned toward the still-open door.

"Could someone give us a ride to Calvin's truck?" Gertrude asked.

"I'll walk to it," Calvin said quickly. "Then I'll come pick you up."

"All right," Gertrude said, not sounding quite satisfied with that plan. She pushed her walker out onto the balcony.

Chip looked at Sandra. "Joyelle told me about her. I'm hoping she's harmless, but ..."

"None of them are harmless," Slaughter said. "No one should be acting like detectives except detectives."

"I'm not acting like a detective—" Sandra started, but then Chip's phone rang.

He looked down at it and then up at Sandra. "Could you give me a minute?"

She nodded and quickly went out onto the balcony. Let him have his private phone conversation. Bob could tell her about it later.

She stood beside Gertrude.

"That cop seems awfully nice for a cop."

Sandra let out a long breath. "I think most cops are nice most of the time."

Gertrude cackled. "Not in Somerset County! Those guys are meaniefaces!"

Sandra bit back a laugh. *Meaniefaces?* Was this woman for real? "Sorry to hear that."

Gertrude looked over her shoulder. "I'm serious. It seems like he doesn't mind if you help. No one wants me to help."

"Sorry to hear that," Sandra said again.

The door opened, and Chip came out onto the balcony. "How far away did your friend park?"

"A good jaunt," Gertrude said. "Do you know Deputy Hale?"

"Somerset Sheriff's Department, right? No, not personally. Why?"

"Just wondering why he's so much meaner than you."

Chip appeared speechless.

"How do you not know him?" Sandra asked. "It's a small state. Does no one get murdered in Somerset County?"

"Not often, no. And Somerset's a lot bigger than this county. Their Sheriff's Department is a lot bigger. They prefer to handle most things on their own, so we let them. If they need help, they call."

A black pickup pulled into the parking lot.

"That's my ride! Hasta la vista!" Gertrude spoke with great excitement but then she moved down the stairs like a snail.

When she finally reached the ground, Chip asked, "How did you get into the apartment?"

She hesitated. "The door was open."

He looked at her. "Was it now?"

She didn't say anything and avoided his eyes.

"That's pretty strange, since I locked it myself after the place was robbed."

"How did you know the place was robbed?"

He didn't answer her, but he did glance at the neighbor's door before tapping on the cover of the book in her hand. "What's that?"

"What was your phone call?"

He smiled. "You first."

She handed the book to him. "I was going to bring this to you. Did you notice that the woman has a high school cheerleading costume on her wall?"

"Costume? You mean it's not real?"

"I have no idea if it's real. I guess I should have called it a uniform. Anyway, you saw it?"

"How could I miss it?"

"Weird, right? Well, then I got to thinking, a woman who frames her cheerleading cos—" She stopped and corrected herself, "cheerleading *uniform* would definitely keep her yearbooks, right? But I didn't see them anywhere. While I was looking for them, I found that book. Weird, right?"

"Why's it weird?"

"Just some random history book about some random town in Michigan? Why would that be on the shelf of a woman who was supposedly born and raised in Maine?"

"What makes you think she was born and raised here?"

"Joyelle said that Jazmyn said so."

Chip handed the book back to her. "You're right. She's not from here. She's from Mount Green, Michigan."

"You knew that?"

"Just found out. That's what that phone call was about. So you can put the book back."

The door opened again, and Slaughter stormed out. "Do you two *mind*?"

Sandra shrank back from her voice.

Chip ignored her. "The neighbor called us." He pointed his thumb over his shoulder. "We thought maybe whoever robbed this place had come back for more."

"Imagine our disappointment," Slaughter said, "when it was only you and your new friends."

"They're not my friends. And you don't know who robbed the place?"

Robin Merrill

"No, do *you*?" Slaughter said.

"Yes. It was Ivan Clark."

Chip pounded on the banister. "Are you serious? How do you know that?"

"Earlier tonight, I saw him in his car, and it was chock-full of women's clothes. I also saw a bunch of framed pictures. I can't swear that it was her stuff, but I'd be willing to bet."

Chip gave her a small smile. "You know, you could've led with that."

Chapter 27

Sandra lay in the dark beside her sleeping husband. She stared at her phone screen. She had searched for Jazmyn Jecks of Mount Green, Michigan, but the results were utter nonsense. She did, however, learn that the small Mount Green High School athletes were indeed the purple and gold mustangs. But there was no online evidence that Jazmyn Jecks had ever been a mustang.

She tried Jazmyn Jecks of Plainfield, Maine, but that produced nothing as well. No social media, at least not under her full name. No police logs. How could a woman like Jazmyn have such a small electronic footprint? That didn't fit with Sandra's mental picture of her. Did she have it all wrong? Was Jazmyn not an attention-seeking glory hound?

Finally, she put the phone down and closed her eyes. But sleep wouldn't come. She felt she was close to figuring this whole thing out but wasn't sure what step to take next. Ivan had to be their guy, didn't he? But how to make sure? She had no idea.

In the morning, after several cups of coffee, she called Chip. "Did you search Ivan's car?"

"Uh ..."

She tapped her toes impatiently. She had to leave soon to get the kids to school.

"Sandra, I appreciate you trying to help, but I can't tell you everything."

What? After he'd been so forthcoming the night before? Had Slaughter read him the riot act?

"And you do know it's not even eight o'clock?"

Yes, she knew that.

"I just woke up."

"Sorry," she said weakly. "I couldn't sleep. I've been worrying about it. I was hoping you'd found her clothes in his car and then arrested him."

"Stop worrying. You don't have to stress about this. You can walk away anytime."

Yeah right. He didn't know she'd promised her help to a dance angel. "I don't want to walk away. I want to help."

"I know you do." He paused. "Look, just take a breather. I'll have a chat with Ivan today. But you stay away from him. I don't think he's dangerous, but you never know."

They said their goodbyes, and then she stared down at her phone, confused.

"What is it, Mum?" Peter asked.

"Detective Buker said that his lead suspect isn't dangerous. Isn't that weird? Aren't murderers, by definition, dangerous?"

He shoved the second half of his Pop-Tart into his mouth. "Maybe he doesn't think he did it." He chewed and swallowed. "Maybe he's not really his lead suspect."

"Maybe," Sandra said thoughtfully.

She herded the kids into the van and took them to school, still mulling the case over in her mind. When she'd dropped them off, she called Joyelle. She didn't want to go home.

Joyelle excitedly agreed to meet her for coffee.

When Sandra told her that Gertrude had fallen into Jazmyn's apartment through a window, Joyelle laughed so hard her latte came out her nose. Sandra handed her one of Sammy's unused napkins. Joyelle thanked her and then daintily dabbed at her face. "I'm so sorry I missed that." She got herself together and then wrapped her hands around her cup and smiled at Sandra. "I can't believe how brave you all are. I would never dare to sneak into someone's apartment in the middle of the night, and yet, all three of you did it!"

Four, actually.

"Maybe you and Gertrude should work together."

"No thank you."

Joyelle laughed again.

"So, did you know that Jazmyn was from Michigan?"

Joyelle frowned. "No, she's not. At least, that's not what she told everyone. She said she was from Aroostook County."

Sandra shook her head. "That's not what Detective Buker says."

"What does he say?" She was so intrigued that Sandra almost laughed.

"Nothing more than that. She moved here from a little town called Mount Green, Michigan."

"Mount Green," Joyelle repeated. "Never heard of it."

"I hadn't either." Sandra took a sip of her coffee.

"Does that mean anything for the case?"

"I don't think so," Sandra said. "It means she was a liar, but I could have assumed that. But I don't think it's more than that. I think Ivan did it, and I doubt he cares anything about her childhood in Mount Green."

"Ivan? He wouldn't kill her. He was in love with her."

Sandra told her about the clothes.

"So, he's still in love with her." Joyelle laughed uncomfortably. "Man, that's creepy."

Sandra felt guilty. "I guess I don't know *for sure* that they were her clothes. But her clothes had been rifled through, and his car was full of sparkly pants." She shrugged and took another drink.

Joyelle scrunched up her face. "I don't mean to argue with you. I know you're good at this, and I know I'm not. But I don't think he did it. Even if she finally got through to him that she wasn't interested, and even if he got mad enough to kill her, I don't think she would have let him into the studio. She wouldn't have let him get close enough to hit her with a trophy."

"Let him in?" Sandra said. "What do you mean? Was the studio locked?"

"I don't know for sure, but I would think so. Jazmyn had a key, but I don't think she would have left the door open if she was in there dancing all alone."

Sandra felt stupid. Of course the door had been locked. Why had she thought otherwise? "Do the police know the door was locked?"

Joyelle shrugged. "I told them what I told you."

"Who else has a key?"

"Now that this has happened, I should probably take all the keys away, make new ones, and stop giving them out. But most of my adult competition dancers have one. They like to come in and practice. A few of them have space to practice at home, but most don't. And most of my adults have kids, so they like to come practice without them. And a few of my serious high school dancers have keys." She folded her lips in. "I think I've given out too many keys."

"Not at all," Sandra said quickly. "There's nothing wrong with being trusting. You're giving them a gift."

"The gift of trust. That's a nice way to look at it."

Sammy threw his sippy cup on the floor, and Joyelle bent to pick it up.

"You don't have to do that," Sandra said, but couldn't even finish her sentence before he threw it again. "Leave it, honestly. He'll play that game forever." Something had made Sandra unsettled, and she couldn't figure out what it was.

Then it came to her, and she inadvertently let out a little gasp.

Joyelle looked up quickly.

Sandra spoke very slowly. "How did you know that Jazmyn was killed with a trophy?"

Joyelle furrowed her brows. "Tell me you're not accusing me of killing one of my dancers."

Sandra shook her head quickly. "No." She hadn't been, had she? Joyelle was far too fabulous to kill anyone. "I was just wondering if the killer had told you about it. I didn't see that detail in the paper or on the news."

Joyelle sighed. "The trophy that was on the shelf right beside where she was killed is missing. I asked the police about it, and they said it was evidence. I then asked them if she'd been killed with a trophy, and they didn't deny it." She sounded ill.

"I'm so sorry this has happened to you and your studio." Sandra wanted to comfort Joyelle. She couldn't imagine how important dance must be to this woman, and to have this ugly, evil thing happen in her studio—how awful. "You know, I haven't thought much about the murder weapon, but now that you mention it, do you know which trophy it was? Was it one of Jazmyn's?"

Joyelle nodded sadly. "Yes, she won a high gold for one of her solo jazz pieces. She was so disappointed. She thought she deserved a higher award."

"Did she?"

Joyelle didn't answer her.

"I think there's some significance there."

"What do you mean?"

"Someone chose to kill her with her own trophy. Was another one of your dancers jealous of her?"

"None of my dancers would kill anyone," she said shortly.

Right. There was that trust again.

"Okay. I'm not saying you're wrong, but were any of them jealous? Maybe Jazmyn said something horrible to one of them, and that person flew into a fit of rage. Maybe they didn't mean to kill her."

"None of my dancers would do that. And she wasn't that good of a dancer. I don't think anyone was jealous of her abilities. I think that trophy just happened to be there, within reach. It is probably a coincidence that they grabbed that one." She took a sip of her latte.

"Maybe."

Joyelle looked thoughtful. "The only person who ever acted jealous of her was Mandi, but that wasn't because of dance. That was because of Ivan."

"Ivan?"

"Yes, Mandi had a thing for Ivan."

The Prima Donna

Sandra shuddered.

Chapter 28

Sandra was going stir crazy. She'd reffed two junior high soccer games, and her legs felt like rubber. She'd fed her family, and they were each busy with their own electronic device. Now she was sitting on the couch staring at an episode of *Father Brown*. She loved this show, especially the Sid scenes, but she hadn't been able to focus and she was totally lost. Father Brown had caught the killer, but Sandra had missed the motive entirely. Maybe she should start carrying an umbrella. Maybe that was his secret. She leaned forward and looked over at her husband. She could slip out and do some investigating, and he wouldn't even notice. But investigate what? She had no leads.

No one cared about Jazmyn Jecks enough to kill her. She stood up abruptly. "I'm going for a drive."

Nate finally looked up. "Oh no."

"What?" She feigned innocence.

"Is Bob going with you?"

"I don't know. I could invite him."

"Yes. Invite him." He sat staring at her as if he was waiting for her to text Bob.

She stared back, not sure how to respond.

"Please don't go snooping without him. You promised."

She had promised that, hadn't she? "Well, I don't normally call him unless it's an emergency. I mean, he's an *angel.* He has other things to do."

"Please." He seemed so sincere that she relented.

She closed her eyes and thought, "God, sorry to bother you. Is Bob available?"

"Meet you in the van."

She jumped.

"What?" Nate asked.

"Bob is in the van."

"Really? It's that easy?"

"Not usually, no," she said, remembering her time alone in the trunk. "Sometimes he's busy." She leaned over and kissed her husband on the top of the head. "Don't wait up and don't worry." She grabbed her phone and her purse and just as Joanna realized she was leaving and started to freak out, she closed the door behind her. She hurried down the steps and climbed into the van, a little embarrassed at how excited she was.

Bob greeted her.

"What, were you just waiting by the phone?"

He laughed. "No, I finished another task minutes ago and was on my way to check in with you."

"Oh."

"So, what have you learned?"

She groaned. "Precious little." She filled him in on everything Joyelle had shared with her.

"So, where are we going?"

"I thought we'd go see Ivan."

"See him? What does that mean, exactly?"

"I don't really know. But I didn't know what else to do. I thought maybe we could just see what he's doing, see if he's up to anything suspicious."

"You're the only one who thinks he's guilty."

"I can't be."

"I think you are. The police certainly have no interest in him."

"He had *her clothes in his car*," Sandra said as if that explained everything. "And this morning Chip said he would check the car."

"And did he?"

"I have no idea."

"Where are we going?"

"I searched his name online, and public records said he was the 'presumed owner of 125 Presley Road.'"

"Online records like that are a really bad idea. Any creepazoid can look up anyone and then go stand at the end of their driveway."

"Did you just call me a *creepazoid*? And I'm not going to stand at the end of his driveway. I have a minivan."

"Presley Road, Presley Road … there is no Presley Road in Plainfield."

"No, he lives in Phillips."

"Phillips?" Bob cried. "We're going all the way to Phillips?"

"Unless you have a better idea. I don't know how else to proceed. I did what you asked. I befriended Joyelle, and we're like real friends now." She realized she was delighted by this development. "But Joyelle doesn't know anything."

"Are you sure?"

"I'm sure. She wants this solved more than anyone. But I can't just sit around doing nothing. I can't, or …" Her voice trailed off.

"Or what?"

"Nothing."

"Or Gertrude will solve it before you?"

"I wasn't going to say that." That's not what she'd been thinking, was it?

"Sure. Anyway, Sandra, sorry, I've got a coach in a bad situation with an athlete. I'll meet you in Phillips." Boom, gone.

She wondered if he really had a job to do or if he wanted to avoid the ride to Phillips. She decided it was probably the former as she didn't think angels lied. Missing the ride to Phillips was just icing on his cake. She turned up the Casting Crowns and sang her way north.

Chapter 29

At the exact second Sandra's minivan crossed the Phillips town line, Bob reappeared in the front seat.

"How do you do the things you do?" Sandra muttered.

"You ain't seen nothin' yet."

"Is the coach situation okay?"

"Not really, but it's calm for now."

They rode in silence for a few minutes, and then she turned onto Presley Road and slowed down so she could see the numbers on the mailboxes.

"We're not even close yet," Bob said.

She sped up a little.

"What are you planning to do when we get there?" he asked.

"I don't know. I think I'm going to drive by."

"Drive by? We came all the way to Phillips to drive by?"

She rolled her eyes, which she might not have done if she thought he could see her. Then she panicked, thinking he could sense that she'd rolled her eyes.

If he could, he didn't let on. "I think the next one is it."

She slowed down again. The house was nearly dilapidated. It looked like a mobile home that had received several additions over the years. On one addition, the roof was sagging badly. Part of the house had siding; part didn't. The yard was fenced in, but part of the fence was missing. The grass was waist-high. She felt sorry for Ivan Clark. Maybe he'd taken the clothes to sell them.

"Stop," Bob said. "Something's wrong."

An outside light was on. The front door stood open, but there were no lights on inside.

She stopped. "You want me to stop here? In the road?"

"We're in Phillips," he whispered. "What are the chances of someone coming along?"

Nevertheless, she attempted to pull onto the nonexistent shoulder and ended up with one tire in the ditch.

"I told you so." He was staring at the house.

She stared at it too, trying to see what he saw. "What's wrong?"

"Not sure. I'll go take a look."

He was gone, and she was annoyed. She stared worriedly at the door of the house, like a dog who'd been left behind in a grocery store parking lot. Soon, he appeared in the doorway and waved to her.

She climbed out of the van.

"You'd better call Chip," he said loudly.

Though she had a pretty good idea why she should call Chip, she asked why anyway.

"Iven Clark is dead. He's been murdered."

She dialed Chip's number and gave him the news.

"What are you doing there?" he cried. "It's the middle of the night!"

This was an exaggeration. "Couldn't sleep."

"Are you safe?" He sounded both irritated and worried.

"Yes." She was quite safe. She was with an angel. She wished she could tell him that. He'd still be irritated, but he'd be less worried.

"Lock yourself in your van. I'll be there in an hour."

"An hour?"

"Yes! I don't live in Franklin County, you know. Anyway"—he sounded out of breath—"if you don't feel safe, you can drive away. But you have to let me know where you're going. Otherwise, sit still until I get there. I'll get there as fast as I can."

"All right. I'll sit still."

"Good. Now, what did you see?"

Oh no. She hadn't seen anything. She hurried toward the door.

"Hello? Are you there?"

"Yes, I'm here." She was inside now, but she couldn't see anything. Her angel friend hadn't turned on the lights.

"Good. Don't go silent on me like that. Now, what did you see?"

She felt around on the wall for a light switch. Her middle finger touched something gooey and she let out a little shriek.

"What? What is it?"

"Nothing," she said quickly. "A bug." She was fairly certain that hadn't been a bug. "Sorry."

Bob turned the lights on.

She gasped.

"He's on the kitchen floor."

Chip hesitated. "Are you looking at him right now?"

"Maybe."

"I told you to get in the car!"

"I will, I will. He's been shot."

"Are you sure he's dead?"

She looked up at Bob, who nodded. "Yeah, I'm sure. Did you ever talk to him about the clothes?"

"Oh, good grief. Even now you're trying to figure things out?"

"Of course I'm trying now. This is the best time to try! I'm standing here staring at a dead body! Did you ask him or not?"

"No, I didn't get to that yet. I have other cases, you know."

She didn't say anything.

"Do you see a gun?" he asked, sounding calmer.

She looked around the cluttered space. "No."

"All right. I'm hanging up now. Call me back if you need me. Now, *go get in your car.*"

Chapter 30

Sandra turned away from the lifeless body of poor Ivan Clark and stepped into his small, cluttered living room. He had a lot of furniture for a man who lived alone. Her heart started pounding. *Did* he live alone? Why had she assumed that? Had his wife or girlfriend shot him because he'd brought home a pile of some other woman's dresses? "Maybe we should go wait in the car," she said, her voice shaky. Even as she finished the sentence, she knew she would do no such thing.

"Go ahead," Bob said. He too knew she wouldn't do it.

Leaving the living room, she stepped into a narrow hallway. The dark paneling on both walls made it feel even darker than it was. It smelled like mildew and sewage. She put the back of her hand to her nose, grateful for the lavender soap she used at home. She paused at a door to her left. Lest she encounter any more surprise goo, she pulled her shirt sleeve down over her hand and turned the doorknob.

The door opened to reveal a relatively neat, sparsely furnished guest room. The mattress was bare, and a few dusty boxes were scattered around the room. She stepped inside, briefly, but she got the sense no one had been in this room for a long time, and she backed out again.

The next door was to her right, and it stood open. She looked into the room.

"Watch your step," Bob said and then reached past her to turn on the light.

Sure enough, there was a large, awkward step down into this room, which was spacious and neater than the rest of the house had been thus far. She walked toward the piano, which was covered with framed pictures of Jazmyn. In most of them, she was dancing. She looked beautiful.

A few of the photos were blurry. Sandra assumed they had been snapped from a distance.

The piano was clean and gleaming. Had Ivan sat here alone, serenading these pictures? The more she knew about the man, the sadder he got.

She looked around the room for another minute and then hiked herself back up into the trailer and turned right to go down the hallway, past the bathroom, which she didn't explore, and into his bedroom.

"I found the clothes," she said.

"I know."

She jumped. She hadn't known that Bob was right behind her.

Shiny dresses, sweaters, sequined costumes, and leggings of every color were piled up on the bed. An imprint in the middle of the collection suggested Ivan had slept among them, probably covered up by them.

"Someone's here," Bob said.

Really? She hadn't heard anything. She followed him back into the living room. "Is it Chip?" This was wishful thinking. No way could he have gotten there already.

"It's Gertrude."

Well, that was better than a murderous wife or girlfriend. Sort of.

"Why are you always everywhere I want to be?" Gertrude cried out when she saw Sandra in the doorway.

"The police are on their way. Ivan is in here. He's dead."

Gertrude stopped ten feet shy of the door and narrowed her eyes. "Did you kill him?"

"Of course not!"

Gertrude started again.

"You can't come in. Detective Buker told me to not let anyone in." This was a lie, but for once, Sandra didn't feel guilty.

Gertrude stopped and glared at her. "Are you going to try to stop me?"

Sandra widened her stance. She had no idea what she was going to do if Gertrude tried to wrestle her way into the house. She didn't want to hurt the obnoxious woman. But was she so sure that was the way such a struggle would go? "Yes, I am."

Slowly, Gertrude started toward her. Sandra's body tensed up, but it took so long for Gertrude to reach her that her body grew tired and started to relax. When Gertrude was within spitting distance, Calvin said, "Gertrude, don't." But it was plain he didn't believe his words held any power over Gertrude.

Gertrude reached the bottom of the steps. Sandra stood on the threshold. The steps were small and narrow and difficult to navigate with a walker. Gertrude stopped to study them. She placed the front legs of her walker on the bottom step, but then there really wasn't any room for her feet. So she moved the walker up another step and then stepped onto the first step. She looked up at Sandra then, as if Sandra should be threatened by her progress.

Sandra was not. Sandra was trying not to laugh. At this rate, Chip would be there before Gertrude got to the top of the steps.

But now that Gertrude had a method, she picked up speed. She was now moving at the speed of a turtle instead of a sloth.

She stopped. She had gone as far as she could go. Because she was standing two steps below Sandra and because Gertrude was short, she was eye level with Sandra's belly button. Sandra brimmed with confidence.

But then Gertrude's demeanor changed. She puffed out her cheeks and picked up her walker and started to pivot on the step, holding her walker a few inches above the porch. What was she doing? She was turning around. Had she given up? She now faced Calvin on the walkway. She put her walker back down on a lower step, but her feet did not descend. Instead, she stepped backward. Her arms pushed up on the walker handles and suddenly she was on the top step, almost touching her. And then she was touching her. She'd moved the walker up another step and was pushing off it with her arms. She bent over a little and shoved her fanny right into Sandra's thighs.

Sandra almost staggered backward and grabbed the frame for support. *Is she boxing me out?* Had this woman played basketball at some point in her life? Sandra really wished she had a whistle to blow.

"Ger*truuuuuude*!" Calvin tried, but Gertrude kept pushing. She was incredibly strong. So much stronger than she looked.

Sandra's hand slipped on the rotten wood, and when she lurched back to get her grip again, Gertrude's body had filled the space. Oh no, Gertrude had a foot on the threshold. And Sandra only had one foot and one hand in place.

Gertrude grunted with effort.

"Oh, just let her in," Bob said, amused.

"A little help would be nice!" she snapped.

Gertrude stopped pushing. "Who are you talking to?" Sandra tried to take advantage of this lull in the action, but then Gertrude came back with a vengeance, slamming her backside into Sandra and placing her second foot on the threshold.

Sandra knew she had lost. She could have kneed the woman in the rump. She could have let go of the house and pushed her back out onto the steps. But she did neither of these things. The woman was obnoxious, but she wasn't evil. And besides, she was older than Sandra. Sandra didn't make a habit of beating up her elders.

Sandra tried to stand her ground, but she could feel her fingers slipping from the weak, splintered wood. Gertrude let out a mighty final grunt, and then Sandra was falling backward. She landed on her rump but had only a second to be angry about the pain of that, because Gertrude was falling toward her. Sandra tried to get her arms up to stop the avalanche of Gertrude, but she didn't have time, and then Gertrude landed on her like a ton of bricks.

Bob was laughing.

"Help," Sandra tried but it came out a wheezy whisper. She tried to roll to the left, but Gertrude had the same idea at the same time. She rolled off Sandra and landed on the floor right in front of her, giving an elbow to Sandra's cheekbone in the process.

"Ow." Sandra's eyes filled with tears.

Gertrude grabbed a rung of her walker and tried to pull herself to her feet.

Sandra realized Calvin was in the house now. He tried to help Gertrude up, but she yanked away from him. "I can do it," she snapped.

Why did this man spend any time with Gertrude at all? Did she have something on him?

Sandra lay there for a minute, trying to recover and wishing Bob would help her up. But the help didn't come. Then Sandra realized she was lying on a filthy floor only feet away from a dead body, and that was all the motivation she needed. When she sat up, Calvin came to her aid and helped her the rest of the way to her feet. She felt guilty accepting help from him. He was no spring chicken either. She gave Bob a dirty look.

Gertrude's eyes snapped to Bob. "Who's there?" she demanded.

"No one is here," Sandra managed, still having trouble breathing.

Gertrude glared at her. "You were asking for help. Who were you talking to?"

"She was probably talking to me, Gertrude," Calvin said.

Gertrude turned to glare at him. "Why would you help her?"

Calvin shrugged. "She's probably wondering why I would help *you*."

Chapter 31

Gertrude inspected Ivan Clark's home in much the same fashion as Sandra had done, only more slowly, and Calvin, Sandra, and Bob followed her around like ducklings.

When she reached the bedroom, she gasped. "Did this fella like to dress up in lady clothes?"

"No," Sandra said quickly. Finally, she had one up on Gertrude. "Those are Jazmyn's clothes. He stole them."

Gertrude shook her head. "What a weirdo." She went to his bureau and then leaned over her walker to open his bottom drawer.

Sandra was impressed she could reach it. She was more flexible than she looked.

"Yep. All man britches in here." She closed the drawer and opened the one above it.

Sandra flinched. She wasn't sure they should be doing this. The man had just died. Did they have the right to rummage through his things? Weren't they dishonoring him? Violating his space? Funny, she hadn't had the same qualms about Jazmyn's home. Was that because of the Aroma Joe's incident? No, she told herself. Jazmyn had been dead for days when they'd entered her apartment. Ivan's body was still in his kitchen. The poor man. He'd been an oddball, but he hadn't deserved that.

Looking disappointed, Gertrude closed the middle drawer and opened the top one.

"Maybe we should wait for the police," Sandra said.

Gertrude snorted. "No. They'll ruin everything."

Sandra didn't know what she meant exactly. Ruin everything? Ruin what? "Their forensics team probably doesn't want us touching everything."

Gertrude ignored her. She reached in and felt around above the drawer.

"We could be destroying evidence that could help them find the killer." *The killer.* As she spoke the words, the reality of the situation felt heavy on her shoulders. This could no longer be about some temper tantrum in a dance studio. There were now two dead bodies. Two people's lives ended. Jazmyn's death hadn't been an accident. The killer was really a killer. A cold-blooded, intentional murderer.

Not finding anything, Gertrude stepped back and then yanked the drawer out of the dresser and flipped it over to look at the bottom. Oh boy.

"Gertrude, she's right," Calvin said, "and you know it." He stepped into the bedroom for the first time. "These cops don't know you. You could get into even more trouble. They're the *State Police*."

Sandra looked at him. "Has she been in trouble with the police before?"

Calvin closed his eyes. "You have no idea."

"They threw me in the clink." Gertrude dropped the drawer on the floor and moved to the drawer beside it. She repeated her whole process.

"What are you *looking* for?" Sandra cried.

"I'll know that when I find out."

What? This woman didn't even make sense. This drawer was also unfruitful, and Gertrude dropped it to the thin carpet, scattering the man's neatly folded socks all over the floor.

"Gertrude, have some respect!" Sandra said.

"No, thank you." Gertrude turned and traveled to his nightstand. She sat on his bed, right in Jazmyn's clothes, and let out a long sigh, as if she was exhausted from all her searching. She pulled open his nightstand drawer. Sandra braced herself, waiting for her to yank it all the way out, but she didn't. Not yet, anyway. She pulled out a pill bottle, and then another, and then another. Soon there were seven carefully-inspected-by-Gertrude, small, brown bottles on the nightstand. Gertrude whistled. "That's a lot of remedies." She bent over to look on the small shelf on the bottom of the nightstand. She picked up a hardcover book. "This book has a *lot* of pages." She shook it like it was a cereal box and she was trying to guess the prize.

This woman was nuts.

She looked at the cover. "*Under the Dome*," she read aloud. "Sounds long." She flipped it open and pulled out the piece of paper that served as a bookmark. Then she snapped the book shut. Sandra winced at the crime of such an act but then realized Ivan probably wouldn't be returning to the book.

Bob stepped up alongside Sandra. "Her investigative style sure does differ from ours."

It made Sandra's heart warm to hear him use the word *ours*. "Mm-hm," Sandra agreed.

Gertrude's head snapped up. "What?"

"Nothing."

Obviously suspicious, Gertrude slowly returned her attention to the piece of paper in her hand.

"It's as if she has no idea what she's doing so she just does everything," Bob said. "Asks everyone, looks everywhere. There's no method to it. No logic."

"Seems to be working, though," Sandra said.

Gertrude looked up again. "Who are you talking to?"

"You." Sandra folded her arms across her chest. "I was talking to you." She was enjoying how frustrated Gertrude was getting with the invisible friend. A small voice told her to stop messing with the woman, but she ignored that voice.

"What seems to be working?" Gertrude asked.

"The furnace." Might as well return nonsense for nonsense.

Gertrude scowled. "You're a little touched, aren't ya?"

Sandra shrugged.

"Keep an eye on her, Calvin. I don't trust her." Gertrude returned her attention to the paper. "Who is Donna Smith?"

"Donna Smith?" Sandra repeated. "I have no idea. Why, what is that?"

Gertrude yanked the paper to her stomach and covered it with both hands. "Wouldn't you like to know?"

"Oh for Pete's sake. Don't worry. I'll give you all the credit for finding it." She would definitely make it clear to Chip who had trashed Ivan's bedroom.

Gertrude's face lit up. "You promise?"

Sandra bit back a laugh. She held up three fingers. "Girl Scout Promise."

Gertrude cackled. "You? A Girl Scout? I highly doubt that!"

Sandra shook her head. Gertrude acted as though she'd claimed to have played with The Rolling Stones. It was true, though. She'd never been a Girl Scout. She *had*, however, volunteered as Assistant Troop Leader last year when Joanna had wanted to be a Brownie. She thought that should count for something. "What is on that paper?" She considered tackling Gertrude and wrestling it out of her hands. Despite their previous encounter, Sandra still thought she could take her.

"It's a photocopy of a mug shot."

"A mug shot?" That *was* interesting. "Of Donna Smith?" Why would Ivan have used a mug shot of some random woman as a bookmark?

"It *says* Donna Smith …" Gertrude turned the paper around so Sandra could see it.

Bob gasped.

"… but it sure looks like our Jazmyn Jecks."

"Maybe she got arrested and gave a fake name," Calvin said.

Sandra remembered what Chip had said when he'd looked at Jazmyn's driver's license. "Or maybe Donna Smith is her real name, and Jazmyn Jecks is the fake name."

Chapter 32

Sandra whipped out her phone and searched for Donna Smith.

"I don't think you're going to have a signal," Bob said. "We're in Phillips, remember."

Bob was right.

"I don't have a signal, but it looks like Ivan's Wi-Fi is open." She connected to it and completed her search.

There were seventy-thousand Donna Smiths in the world. "Uh, I think the name is too common."

"Try Donna Smith in Maine," Gertrude said, getting up and coming to stand uncomfortably close to Sandra.

Sandra resisted the urge to sidestep away from her. She didn't want to be rude, for one, but also, that would put her right up against the wall, and she knew Gertrude would just come closer again. She scrolled through an entire page of obituaries with Gertrude leaning over her arm to peer at her phone. The second page gave them a living masseuse by that name and then a living personal injury lawyer. Sandra didn't think Jazmyn had ever been either of those things. She couldn't picture her healing anyone or graduating from law school. She kept scrolling. An ancestry website featured a Donna Smith of Maine who had been born in 1876. Sandra didn't think that was her either. Then she was out of Maine Donna Smiths.

"Try Michigan," Bob said.

She replaced "Maine" with "Michigan" in the search bar.

"Michigan?" Gertrude cried. "Why Michigan?" She leaned away from Sandra. "Do you know something I don't know?"

Sandra didn't answer her. She decided to try pretending Gertrude wasn't there.

Sandra and Gertrude gasped in unison. "Oh no," Sandra said.

"What is it?" Calvin said.

"Mount Green Drunk Driver Charged With Vehicular Homicide." Sandra read the headline aloud and then scanned the article. "There's no picture, but a woman named Donna Smith hit a woman named Shawna Pevzner. It says Ms. Smith failed to maintain lane, that she drove onto the sidewalk and hit the victim. Ms. Smith did not stop, did not help, and did not call for help." Sandra shuddered at the thought. "She fled the scene," she said softly.

"Then what?" Bob asked.

"Then I don't know. That's all the article says. Hang on." Sandra searched for "Mount Green Donna Smith trial."

Calvin and Bob stepped closer too. Sandra felt claustrophobic. She needed a bigger phone.

She found the article about the trial. The text was brief, but the picture was damning. "It's her, all right." She looked younger and less bling-bling, but it was her. "It says she got five years."

"When did she get out?" Bob asked.

Sandra did another search. "I don't know, but the accident happened in 2012. She was eighteen. So add a year maybe for the trial and then five years for the sentence ... maybe she moved to Maine in 2018?"

"I doubt she served the full five years," Calvin said. "They are always letting criminals off easy and letting them out early."

"Maybe," Sandra said, a little startled by Calvin's harsh tone. He'd seemed like such a nice man. She didn't think it mattered when Donna-Jazmyn had moved to Maine. "I'm not sure any of this has anything to do with her death? I mean, that happened in Michigan. And what would that have to do with Ivan?" As soon as she asked the question, she had an answer. "*Unless* he was killed because he found out she was Donna Smith."

"That doesn't make any sense," Gertrude said. "If Jazmyn had killed him because he found out about her past, I would agree with you. But she obviously didn't kill him."

"Wait," Sandra said. Her thoughts were coming together like puzzle pieces. "If someone killed Jazmyn because of this thing in Michigan, then that someone really wouldn't be happy to know that Ivan knew about Michigan."

"That's true," Bob said.

Gertrude wasn't following.

"Let's say that Shawna Pevzner's loved one decided to hunt down Donna Smith and get some revenge. And then he or she finds out that Ivan knew about the Michigan crime? Wouldn't that knowledge lead to them being caught? So maybe they killed Ivan so the cops wouldn't learn about the Michigan connection?"

They heard sirens. Gertrude hurriedly shoved the photocopy into her bulging walker pouch.

"Gertrude, I'm going to tell them what we've found."

Gertrude gasped. "You wouldn't!"

Chapter 33

Chip stepped into the trailer and grimaced when he saw Gertrude. Then he looked at Sandra. "I thought I told you to wait in your car."

"I was trying to stop her from entering and mucking up your crime scene."

Chip smirked. "Nice work."

"Sorry." Sandra was embarrassed. "She's stronger than she looks."

Chip stepped aside. "Leave now. All three of you."

"Hang on, Chip. We found something." Sandra looked at Gertrude. "Show him."

"Show him what? I didn't find anything!"

Sandra rolled her eyes. "Gertrude has been touching everything, so you might want to fingerprint her. Anyway, she found a photocopy of a mug shot for a Donna Smith of Mount Green, Michigan—"

Chip held up his hand. "Are you about to tell me that Jazmyn Jecks's real name is Donna Smith?"

"Yes," Sandra said sheepishly.

"We know that."

"How do you know that?" Gertrude cried.

"We're the police."

Slaughter stepped inside. The trailer suddenly felt too small, and Sandra stepped outside. Then she turned back toward Chip. "Do you think it's connected? Do you think the Michigan crime has something to do with her death?"

"We have no reason to think that, but we're not ruling anything out." Chip hesitated. "Did you see anything else I should know about?"

Sandra shook her head. "He's got her pictures everywhere. A lot of them look like he took them from afar. And he moved her clothes from his car to his bed."

Chip nodded thoughtfully. "Okay, thank you. You can go home."

Sandra turned to go down the steps.

Gertrude hurried after her. "Why are they so nice to you?"

Sandra shrugged. "I don't know. Why wouldn't they be?"

"Because the cops in my county are bullies. I think I should move to Franklin County."

Oh no, please don't.

"I thought you were moving to South Dakota," Calvin said dryly.

"I am. But Franklin County is a lot closer."

Slaughter called after them, "If it were up to me, you all would be in handcuffs right now."

"There," Gertrude said. "That's more along the lines of what I'm accustomed to. What are you going to do now?"

"Do? I'm going home and going to bed. What are you going to do?"

Gertrude scrunched up her face. "I'm going to keep investigating."

"I'm not sure what else there is to do tonight."

"That's because *you're* not a gumshoe."

Sandra nearly ran to her minivan. Though Gertrude didn't chase after her, she still locked the doors. Part of her wanted to stay behind and see what else she could learn, but she was exhausted. And she was starting to feel a bit extraneous to this case. Chip didn't seem to need her help after all. All she'd done was wander around and learn things that he'd already known.

"What do you think?" Bob asked when she'd gotten her van turned around and pointed toward home.

"I think I'm too tired to think."

"I think you're right. I think all the crimes are connected."

"Thank you."

"For what?"

"For thinking I'm right."

184

"You need to ask Joyelle about this as soon as possible. I hope the police haven't already asked her about it."

"Asked her about the drunk driving conviction?"

"Yes."

"What's the hurry?"

"I want to gauge her reaction. See if she knew. And if she did, we can ask if any of her students knew."

"I am certain she didn't know. She would've mentioned it."

"Please ask her anyway."

"I will, but not tonight."

"Fine." He sounded disappointed. And then he was gone.

Sandra rolled down the window and turned the music up and still she was too tired to be driving safely. She rummaged around in her purse until she found some gum and popped a few pieces in her mouth. There, that was better. Good old sugar.

The more she thought about her theory, the more she thought she was right. So, who had come to Maine to exact their revenge on Donna Smith? And had they already left and gone back to Michigan? If so, she was never going to figure this out. This thought saddened her, so she chose not to believe it. She would operate on the premise that the murderer was still lurking around Franklin County.

Chapter 34

Gertrude entered the dance studio and scampered over to where Sandra was stretching. "Have you learned anything?"

"No," Sandra said grudgingly. It wasn't for lack of trying. Joyelle hadn't been available for coffee since Sandra had found Ivan's body. She wondered if Joyelle was avoiding her. She'd gotten to dance early to try to talk to her, but Joyelle had been swarmed by moms trying to order tights. Apparently, there was a big tights sale going on. "Have you?"

"Have I what?"

"Learned anything?"

"If I had, I wouldn't tell you." Gertrude spun and went across the room to a vacant spot. Then she stopped and waited, silently studying each of the adult dancers.

Tap class was uneventful but then it was time for jazz, and Joyelle pleasantly insisted that Gertrude participate. Sandra could understand her motivation. The others were probably getting suspicious as to why Gertrude was in class if she was just going to stand around. Or maybe they had already figured it out.

Gertrude didn't seem pleased with the directive, but she did start to move her feet a little. Joyelle arranged them in staggered lines. Sandra ended up behind Gertrude, who was between Jess and April, whom Sandra still thought of as Barbie.

They learned four counts of simple steps, and Sandra was impressed that Gertrude was sort of doing them. Then Joyelle asked them to do three turns in a row. Sandra was too focused on her own spinning to pay much attention to the others, and the whole affair made her feel a bit ill.

But the others must have done better than her because Joyelle praised them all. Then as an afterthought, she added, "Don't forget to spot! We don't want you getting dizzy!"

Sandra didn't know what spotting was but she was determined to try it next time because she was indeed dizzy.

Jess turned and smiled broadly at Gertrude. "Spotting means to pick one spot on the wall and keep looking at it so that when you spin, you have a spot to focus on."

"I know what spotting is," Gertrude snapped.

The smile fell off Jess's face.

Joyelle counted them off and again they went through the four-count and into the spins. This time, Sandra kept her eyes on a spot inches above the mirror. This did make spinning easier, and because she was looking up, she was able to see that Gertrude had picked up her walker and was spinning around as fast as she could with her walker held out straight in front of her.

The mother in Sandra sprang to life. "Gertrude! That might be a bit danger—"

As Sandra spoke, Gertrude lost her balance and staggered sideways, still spinning. With a mighty momentum, she clobbered April in her lower back and sent her sprawling face-first onto the floor.

In a bit of a panic, Joyelle stopped the class and rushed to April's side.

Gertrude was still spinning.

Joyelle knelt on one knee. "Are you all right?"

April got up slowly and then smiled sweetly at her assailant, who had finally come to a wobbly halt.

April's reaction was not the one Sandra had been expecting. "Yes, I'm fine." The tears in her eyes suggested that the encounter had hurt—it *had* to have hurt—but she obviously was trying to hide that fact.

Joyelle looked at Gertrude nervously.

"I'm dizzy!" Gertrude said. "Why doesn't anyone care about me?"

Joyelle gave Sandra a bewildered look as if asking for help.

Sandra didn't know what help she could give and so offered none.

Joyelle looked at Gertrude. "I'm going to have to insist that you be more careful, or you won't be able to dance with us."

"You're the one making me dance!"

Joyelle took a deep breath. "You won't be allowed in the studio at all, Gertrude." She returned to the front of the room. "Feel free to take a break, April, if you need to. All right, everyone, let's move on to the next four counts. First, we're going to hold for a full count, give us a chance to gather ourselves. Then, let your legs slide apart as if you're going into a split, but don't panic! We are not really going into a split. As you get lower, put your hands out and lower your stomach to the floor. As you do that, slide your legs back so they lie straight out behind you."

"We're going to lie down in dance class?" Gertrude exclaimed.

A few of the dancers give Gertrude a dirty look. She was wearing on them.

"This is part of the dance, Gertrude," Joyelle said as if she were talking to one of her kindergarten students. "Here. I'll show you." Gracefully, Joyelle lowered herself to the floor. It looked beautiful. Sandra couldn't imagine what it was about to look like for Gertrude and her.

Joyelle bounced back to her feet and said, "All right, let's try it. Don't worry about how it goes your first time."

Sandra had intended to participate in this part of class, but she was quickly distracted by Gertrude, whose feet—Sandra noted that today she was wearing two socks—rapidly slid apart, sending her sprawling into a split. Gertrude cried out in pain as the top half of her hurtled toward the hardwood. Trying to hang on to her walker, she didn't put her hands out to break her fall. But the force of the impact caused her to let go of the walker after all, and it skittered away from her as if trying to escape the calamity.

Several of the women in the class started laughing, and Joyelle gave them a scalding look. "That's a great try, Gertrude! You just went down a little too quickly."

Way too quickly. How worn out were the bottoms of her sneakers to allow a spill like that? Sandra considered getting Gertrude some new tennis shoes from the clothing closet at church.

Gertrude rolled over onto her back, her face twisted in pain. She tried to sit up but then fell back again. "I'm stuck!" She held both hands up in the air as if expecting someone to grab them and hoist her back to her feet. Sandra wondered if she should go find Calvin. Was he sitting in the parking lot? He should be here for this.

"Is someone going to help me?" Gertrude demanded and shook her hands furiously in the air. *Jazz hands*, Sandra thought and then bit her lip to keep from smiling.

April went to her then, grabbed hold of her hands, and tried to pull her to her feet, but still, Gertrude didn't move. Jess went to help too, and Sandra felt guilty that she hadn't volunteered. Jess took one arm, and April took the other, and together, looking like they were trying to pull a wagon out of deep mud, they managed to pull Gertrude to her feet.

Beyond flustered, Joyelle announced that it was time for a drink break. It was the first time Sandra had ever heard her give a drink break in the middle of class. People broke into small clusters, and only a few of them went for hydration. The rest of them sneaked furtive glances at Gertrude and snickered to each other.

Looking regretful, Joyelle called them back and said, "Now, I don't want to try this part right now, but the next four counts we're going to push up with our arms and do a little jump to bring our feet underneath us. Then we're going to jump to our feet and put our arms in the air. Then, slowly bring your arms down as you merge the two lines into one.

"Next, on the one-two count, put your right arm around the shoulders of the dancer to your right. Then on the three-four count, put your left arm around the shoulders of the person on your left. All right." She looked terrified. "Let's just try that part. Merge yourselves into one line." She started to count, and most of the women put their right arms over the shoulders to the right, as they were supposed to.

"I can't do this!" Gertrude cried. "I can't let go of my walker!"

It seemed Joyelle had been anticipating this reaction. "That's okay, Gertrude. The people on either side of you will put their arms around your shoulders."

The women linked together. "Now, small step with your right foot and then, turning your body slightly to the right, kick up with your left. Follow the beat and you'll stay together. Then a small step forward with your left and kick up with your right, while turning your body a little bit to the left." Most of the women followed the instructions as she spoke them. "Great! Perfect, that's it. For those of you who haven't done this before, just watch Jess and April. Follow them. All right, let's try it from the top. Here we go, 5 … 6 … 7 … 8 …" All the women turned slightly to the right and brought their left legs into the air almost in unison.

Gertrude grunted and lifted her left foot approximately six inches off the ground. Her foot smashed into her walker, and she let out a small cry of pain. Then she pushed her walker forward a foot, turned her body to the left, and kicked her right leg, again six inches into the air. Again she kicked the walker, and again she cried out in pain. Another foot forward, turned her body to the right, brought her left foot up again, and kicked the walker again.

"Stop!" Joyelle nearly screamed. "That's all for today. Take another break, and then we'll come back for ballet."

Sandra didn't know whether to laugh or cry.

The women filed out of the room to change their shoes, and Gertrude came straight for her. There was no need for Gertrude to change her shoes because she did everything in her sneakers. "What do you think about Mandi?" Gertrude asked her as if none of the preceding incidents had taken place.

"Mandi? What about her?"

"She is suspicious."

"How so?"

"Are you blind? She's been crying all class!"

She has? Sandra hadn't noticed. She'd been too busy watching Gertrude try to dance. "I don't know, but women cry for lots of reasons. Doesn't mean it has anything to do with Jazmyn's death."

"Everything has to do with everything, Sandra," Gertrude said and then turned and left the room.

Sandra looked at Joyelle. "We have to figure this out. Soon."

Chapter 35

"You danced good, Mama," Joanna said, buckling her seatbelt.

"Thank you, honey. So did you. But we danced *well*, not *good*."

Joanna groaned. Then she chirped, "Hi, Bob."

Sandra jumped. She hadn't known he was there. "Well hello, stranger."

"What've we got?"

"We? Where have you been?"

Bob raised an eyebrow. "Do you really need an angelic force at dance class?"

"I guess not."

"There was a dust-up at the Lawrence football practice."

"I'm sorry to hear that."

"And I've been keeping an eye on Chip and Slaughter, see if I can learn anything."

"And?"

"And nothing. They don't know anything. They found no interesting prints at Ivan's house and no murder weapon. But he was killed with a two-forty-three."

"A what?"

"That was the caliber size. The bullet."

"Oh." Sandra didn't know anything about bullets.

"They seemed surprised by that, but I don't know why."

She glanced at him. "Angels don't know guns?"

"The hunting angels do. The military angels do. This middle school sports angel does not. But I know how much psi is supposed to be in a soccer ball, and they don't."

She held up a hand. "I wasn't picking on you. I was only curious."

"And I know the free throw percentage for every kid in my territory!" He was still defensive.

Why on earth would he know that? Why would anyone ever need to know that? She thought it best to change the subject. "We need to talk to someone who knows what a two-forty-three is."

"Maybe Gertrude knows."

"No!" she said quickly with less decorum than she would've liked. "I don't think Gertrude knows anything about bullets."

He snickered. "You don't want her to know something you don't know."

"Have you *seen* the woman? What makes you think she knows anything about bullets?"

"Fine. Who do you want to ask?"

"Did you look it up online?"

He laughed. "Of course not. Angels don't do that."

"What do angels do?"

He didn't answer her.

"We could ask the hunting angel?"

"It's bow season. He's very busy."

Frustration was creeping in. "Fine." She pulled the van into the next available parking lot, which, she realized too late, was a bar.

"Yes, these people might know."

She rolled her eyes in the darkness. "We're not going in." She fished out her phone and started to type. "What did you say it was again?"

"Two-forty-three," he said slowly.

She waited for results and then read them aloud. "The .243 Winchester is a sporting rifle cartridge originally designed for target practice or varmint shooting. Today it is used to hunt coyotes, deer, and wild hogs." She looked up at him. "Sounds pretty common. I don't know why that would be surprising to them."

Bob shrugged. "Maybe we should go in there and ask." He pointed his chin at the door under the neon beer sign.

"No! Stop it!"

His face fell. He looked like Peter looked when Sandra told him to turn off his video games.

"If you want to go in, go ahead in."

He appeared to be thinking about it.

She hoped he would decide against it. She didn't want him doing any more investigating without her.

A man came out of the bar, lit a cigarette, and headed toward a pickup.

"Go ask him," Bob said.

"I'm not walking up to some strange man in a bar's dark parking lot!"

"Fine." He was upset with her.

"Can't we wait until tomorrow and go talk to someone at a gun store?"

Bob shook his head. "It would be so much faster to go ask that guy."

The man hadn't gotten into his truck. He was leaning against the driver's side door, smoking his cigarette.

"Come on. Time is a factor here. We need an answer. I'll be right here the whole time. Nothing bad will happen."

She sighed. "Fine. But I'm not going to get out of the van."

"Fine."

"Fine." She looked in the rearview. "Joanna, duck down."

Joanna hesitated. "You really want me to?"

"Yes!" She sounded less patient than she'd meant to. Bob's directive was so absurd that she was freaking out a little.

Joanna ducked down.

Still feeling that this was a bad idea, Sandra drove across the parking lot. She rolled down her window. "Excuse me?"

He looked up at her.

Good. He looked normal enough. Probably not a serial killer.

Chapter 36

Sandra's heart was racing. This was so stupid. She hesitated. How could she ask a stranger in a bar's dark parking lot a hypothetical question about shooting someone without sounding like she was planning to shoot someone? "I know this is weird, but it's driving me crazy. Someone told me that a man had been killed with a ..." She forgot the numbers again.

"Two forty-three," Bob said quickly.

"Two forty-three," she repeated, "and everyone was all surprised at that. Do you know why?"

The parking lot lights were few and dim, and the brim of his baseball cap cast an extra shadow on his face. She couldn't tell if he was confused, annoyed, or angry. "What makes you think I'd know?" He looked into the van as if he could sense someone else was in there.

"I'm alone," she said quickly, thinking of Joanna. Since she'd already lied once, she figured she might as well continue. "I pulled in here to finish a phone call, you know, want to be safe and all ..." She tittered and it sounded manic. Her cheeks were on fire. She was grateful for the dark. "And my friend told me about the gun, and it was really bothering me.

It's weird, I know, but I saw you and thought you'd probably know." She paused, wishing for time travel.

"Be calm," Bob said, "you're doing fine."

She wanted to snap at him that she was most definitely *not* doing fine, but she managed not to.

Something behind her let out a primal shriek. A surge of adrenaline rushed through Sandra. She looked in the rearview mirror. What on earth could make a sound like that, and why had it sounded familiar? She couldn't see anything.

The man in the cap looked into the darkness behind her van. "Calm down. It's nothing. She's just asking me a question about guns." He said this as if it made sense.

"Guns?" the person wailed. Sandra definitely knew that voice but from where? "Why, is she going to shoot you?"

"No! Calm down. Get in the truck."

"Do you *know* her?" she accused.

"No." He sounded exasperated. "I told you, she's just asking me a question—"

"Well, *I* know her! I'd know that van anywhere! I remember the bumper sticker." The fifth-grade honor student bumper sticker.

As proud as she was of her son, she vowed to scrape that sticker off pronto.

Finally, Sandra caught a glimpse of the woman in her side mirror.

Ms. Cowbell.

"Thanks anyway, sorry to bother you," Sandra said to the man as fast as possible.

Ms. Cowbell, who didn't appear to be armed, but Sandra didn't want to take any chances, was fast gaining on her car door. Sandra couldn't back up without hitting her, so she drove her van forward, intending to immediately turn the van around and speed away, but when she swung the van to the right, she couldn't quite make the turn without clipping the trucks parked in the next row. She muttered a semi-naughty word.

"Mom!" Joanna accused from the back.

She threw the van in reverse and backed up two feet. This wasn't going to be a three-point turn. It was going to take at least five.

Ms. Cowbell was still coming. "Are you following me? Are you trying to prove something, stealing *my* boyfriend?" She punctuated that accusation with a few curses of her own.

Sandra put the van in drive again, praying she could make the turn, and she probably could have if she hadn't been so flustered.

"You're more scared right now than you were when you were being chased by a murderer," Bob said.

Sandra threw the van into reverse while it was still rolling forward, and it lurched in protest. "I know, but I know this woman, and she's *crazy*!"

"What did you just say?" Ms. Cowbell screamed. "Who are you talking to? Are you talking to me?"

She backed up a few more inches, wishing she had one of those fancy backup cameras.

"Take a breath," Bob said, and his calmness annoyed her. "I won't let her hurt you."

Maybe not, but she was only feet away from the van now.

Sandra rolled up the window with her left hand, put the car in drive with her right hand, and stomped on the gas with her foot without holding onto the wheel. As her tires found purchase, the nice man's girlfriend swung her giant plastic purse over her head and brought it down like a battle ax. It glanced off the side of the minivan, probably leaving a dent, but Sandra didn't care—there were a thousand dents. Her tires spun up two rooster tails of gravel, which sprayed the surrounding trucks, the owners of which might get more upset about dents than she did. Her embarrassment deepened. She hadn't meant to do that. But she didn't feel bad enough to slow down.

She didn't dare look at Ms. Cowbell, whom she might've injured, but as she drove by Mr. Cowbell, he had turned his body away from her van and brought his arm up to shield his face from the projectiles.

She didn't even slow down to check for traffic. She pulled out onto the road without looking both ways and turned the van so fast that it went up on two tires. At least, that's what it felt like. She didn't feel the other two tires crash back to the asphalt, so maybe that hadn't really happened.

Bob was laughing.

"I am so angry at you!" she hollered at the angel.

"What? I didn't do anything!"

"You had a really lame idea! Did you know that she was there? Did you do that for your own entertainment?"

"Of course not. Angels have far better ways to entertain ourselves. And no, I don't even know who she was."

"You don't? That's the woman who tried to kill Moose and me with a cowbell at Dixville Falls!"

Understanding dawned. "Oh! Now I understand why she was so upset."

Sandra tried to get her breathing under control.

"Why would those two drive all the way from Dixville Falls to drink in Plainfield?" Bob said contemplatively.

"I doubt that's the case. I'm betting he lives here."

"Well then, you better hope they don't hit it off, get married, move to Dixville Falls, and make more soccer players."

She didn't answer him. She was suddenly very tired.

"Mama? Can I get off the floor now?"

Sandra's stomach rolled. "Of course, honey. Get in your seat and buckle up." She'd done it again. Her goofy sleuthing had put her children in danger. Nate was going to have a fit. "I'm so sorry, honey." She needed to solve this case for the dance angel, and then she needed to retire.

Sandra heard the click of the seatbelt.

"That woman said a lot of bad words."

Bob snickered.

"Yes, she did," Sandra said. "I'm sorry you had to hear that."

"It's okay. I hear the same words at school. Just not all at the same time."

Bob laughed again, and this time it was more than a snicker.

Joanna joined him.

The two of them were having a grand time.

"Quiet, both of you," Sandra ordered.

But they kept laughing, each feeding off the other, leaving Sandra to be the only one still wondering why a two-forty-three bullet was a big deal.

Chapter 37

Sandra pulled her van into the tiny parking lot of Beer, Bait, and Bullets. She could hardly call it a parking lot at all. It appeared to be the owner's driveway. She'd never been here before, but from the look of the property, she assumed that he'd built a small building near his home for his gun store. Wondering where on earth Bob was, she slid out of the van and grabbed the handle of the sliding door.

It was stuck. She sighed. Now what. She pulled harder. Nothing. This was not good. She didn't know how much it cost to unstick a sliding van door, and she didn't think she could live with only one rear door. She started around the van to get Sammy out from the other side, but then the van door slid open. She looked around for Bob. "Thank you?" she said quietly, hoping it had been Bob who had done her the favor.

"You're welcome," Bob said, "but don't talk to me right now."

She stuck her head into the van. "Why? Is he watching us?" She glanced toward the store.

"No, the wife is, from the house."

She unhooked Sammy, who thanked her by punching her in the eye with his tiny, slimy fist.

"Was she watching when my van door slid open on its own?"

"Yes, but I didn't realize that until I'd done it. Don't worry. She'll probably think it's an automatic."

"Uh-huh." She straightened up, pulling Sammy out of the van. Then she gently slid the door shut. "Did you fix it or just open it this once?"

"It's fixed."

She looked around. "Will you please show yourself? You're making me nervous."

He appeared right beside her, and she jumped.

"Let's go." She led the way up the steps to the small store and reached for the door handle.

"There's a buzzer."

Oh. She pressed the button, and the door clicked open. She stepped inside and looked around. Whoa. She'd never seen so many guns in one place.

"Can I help you?" a man asked from the front.

"Maybe," she said. She'd vowed to just tell the man the truth, but now she was nervous and was considering lying again. That had gone so well last time. "I'm thinking of buying a two … forty … three." She spoke the numbers slowly, scared of messing them up.

He nodded. "All right. We've got a few of those. Would you like to see one?"

She looked at Bob. She had no idea if she needed to see one. "Sure."

He disappeared for a moment and then returned and laid two guns on the counter.

She didn't get closer.

"You're welcome to handle them."

She stepped closer because she thought that was what she was supposed to do. Sammy squirmed in her arms.

"You can put him down. We get lots of kids in here. He can't get at anything."

She smiled, but she didn't put him down. She thought maybe the kind man was underestimating Sammy. Yes, the guns were all high off the floor, but Sammy was a climber.

"Not what you were expecting?" He read her mind.

"They're both so … big."

He furrowed his brow. "Not really. Have you shot a two-forty-three before?"

She shook her head.

"Nothing to be embarrassed about." He read her mind again. He was good. "We get new shooters in here every day. Can I ask what makes you interested in that caliber?"

She hesitated, unsure how to answer that.

"Don't get me wrong. These are great rifles. I use one just like this one"—he touched one of the rifles—"to hunt deer. Do you hunt?"

She shook her head again.

"Okay." He scratched his jaw and smiled at Sammy, who then reached out to grab him.

Sandra pushed his chubby little arm down.

"That's all right. Most of the women we get in here don't hunt. They're usually more interested in target shooting or self-defense. What do you plan to use your new gun for?"

She didn't know how to answer this, so she didn't. "I thought they would be smaller."

He stared at her, and she felt him analyzing her. "Were you expecting a pistol?" He pointed to a handgun on the counter.

She breathed out a sigh of relief. "Yes, like that."

"Well, the two-forty-three doesn't really come in a pistol. There are smaller versions, but they've got really long barrels, and I don't carry those. I could order you one, but I've got a feeling you don't really want a two-forty-three."

He was very good.

"So, a two-forty-three wouldn't make a good self-defense weapon?"

He shook his head. "It's not most people's first choice. Is that what you're looking for?"

She should have gone with the truth. Why hadn't she done that? "I don't know what I'm looking for. But you're saying a two-forty-three is a hunting gun, and they're usually big?"

He studied her again. "They are almost always rifles."

She nodded. "So no one goes around killing people with a two-forty-three rifle?"

His expression changed. He suddenly looked a little less friendly, and a little more suspicious. "Are you planning on killing someone?"

"No, no, I'm just looking for a safe gun."

His suspicion grew. "All guns are safe when they're in safe hands."

"I know. Sorry, I didn't mean to suggest otherwise. You know what? I sincerely thank you for your time, but I think I need to do more research."

He nodded slowly. "You have a nice day then."

She wasn't confident in the sincerity of this statement. "Thanks." She backed up quickly, taking care not to make as much of a scene with her departure as she had the night before.

"Bye-bye!" Sammy waved.

The man's friendly smile returned. "Bye, little guy."

And then she was outside and trying not to run to her minivan. She strapped Sammy in as fast as she could and got behind the wheel.

"I get it," Bob said.

"Get what?" She started the car.

"Someone went into Ivan Clark's trailer and shot him with a rifle. That is odd. The police usually deal with handgun shootings, so they were surprised that he'd been killed with a rifle."

Bob was right. That was odd. "Why would someone do that?"

He shrugged. "Maybe we're looking for a hunter? Or maybe not. I am certain that around here, hunting rifles are easier to come by than handguns. But they're not easy to hide. Someone walked across his yard and up his steps carrying a big gun."

"But he doesn't have any neighbors close enough to see anything. And there's hardly any traffic on his road."

"True." He looked at her. "I don't know why someone shot him with a rifle. But we now know why the police were surprised."

She grimaced. She didn't think this knowledge was worth the bounty of dignity she'd had to pay in exchange.

Chapter 38

"Let's drop Sammy off at Ethel's," Sandra said.

"All right," Bob said, sounding amused. "Why?"

"I want to see if April is home."

"April? Why?"

"Because if she's not, we can maybe snoop around and see if we can find a gun. I would think it would be hard to hide a gun that big."

"Why April, though? Why is your brain going straight to her?"

"She was weird on Tuesday night. I wish you'd seen it because I know you'd agree with me. Gertrude is so far beyond obnoxious. She literally injured April. And yet, April was as sweet as pie. And when Gertrude fell down, April came rushing over to help. It was bizarre."

Bob stared at her.

"What?"

"You think she's a murderer because she's *nice*?"

"No! It's more of a gut feeling. If you'd seen it, you'd be on my side." She sighed in resignation. "All right. Maybe we don't go to her place. But I'm not sure how to proceed, and that frustrates me. We have no leads. And I don't know how to find one."

"Can we find out if April is from Michigan?"

Sandra almost slapped herself in the forehead. Of course! If Jazmyn—or Donna, whatever her name was—was killed because of the accident in Michigan, then of course the killer would be from Michigan. She pulled the van over.

"What are you doing?" Bob looked out his window at the medicinal marijuana store they were now parked in front of. "Did Ethel move?"

"No, I'm calling Chip."

"Really?"

"Really. We need the crime solved. I don't necessarily need to do it myself." Of course, Sandra wanted to be the first one to crack the case, but more than that, she wanted to make sure Gertrude *wasn't* the first one to crack the case.

Chip answered on the third ring.

"Have you looked into April?" Sandra asked, after the perfunctory pleasantries.

"No. I'm focusing on October for right now."

Sandra tried to gratify his attempt at humor with a fake laugh, but her laugh sounded more like the cry of a startled donkey. "I was being serious."

"So am I. Who is April?"

"I don't know her last name. She's one of the adult dancers at Synergy Dance Studio."

"Why would we look into her? Sandra, I know you mean well, but I'm busy here." The condescending tone of his second sentence erased her motivation to answer his first one. And she could hear Slaughter harping in the background.

"Fine. Sorry to bother you." She hung up.

"That went well."

She sneered at the angel. "I didn't know angels were big on irony."

"Who are you calling now?"

"No one. I'm looking at April's social media profiles." Of course, she wasn't friends with the stranger, so she had to go to Joyelle's page and then find April there, which took a few seconds, and Bob made his impatience clear by tapping on the dashboard. It sounded like a fifth-grade drum solo. She found April's account and scrolled down. She groaned.

"What is it?"

"There is literally no personal information here."

"Smart woman."

"Yes, she is." Maybe *too* smart. "She doesn't even use her last name on here unless her last name is May."

Bob snickered. "Someone named their child April May?"

"Maybe? Maybe not. Lots of fake names around here."

"How do you know where she lives?"

"I don't yet. I was going to ask Joyelle."

Bob stared through the windshield, squinting.

Sandra drove away from the pot shop.

"All right," Bob said. "If we can figure out where she lives, I say we go take a peek. But only because I want to see if she's from Michigan, not because I think we'll find a gun, though that would certainly simplify things. And maybe we should wait until dark."

"I would assume she'd be home at night."

"Why do you assume she's not home right now?"

"She runs a daycare downtown."

"How do you know that?"

"Joyelle told me."

"Oh!" He sounded impressed. She didn't know why. She had accomplished far more impressive sleuthing feats. "All right then. Let's go have a look."

"Can you make me invisible?"

"I don't think that would be a good idea."

"So you *can* make me invisible!" She was unreasonably excited about the idea.

"I didn't say that."

"Actually, you kind of did."

Chapter 39

Having deposited Sammy into Ethel's loving arms, Sandra now sat with Bob in Ethel's driveway. "I'm calling Joyelle."

Bob nodded and gazed out the windshield patiently.

Joyelle answered quickly.

"Hi, Joyelle. Would you mind sharing April's address with me?"

She hesitated. "Why?"

"We just need to ask her some questions." She flinched at her use of the word *we,* but Joyelle didn't mention it. Maybe she thought Gertrude was Sandra's plus one. Sandra shuddered at the thought.

"April lives in the middle of nowhere. Wouldn't it be easier to see her at her work? She should be there now." This was a reasonable suggestion. Joyelle was on to her. She knew she wanted to do more than ask questions.

"That's great. Thanks, Joyelle." She hung up the phone and looked at Bob.

"We should have expected that," he said.

"Maybe. Hey, do a search for April May in Plainfield. Maybe her address will pop up." She didn't have high hopes, but it was worth a shot. It had worked for Ivan Clark, but she didn't think Ivan Clark was hiding out under a new name.

"Nothing," Bob said. "The world wide web thinks I'm shopping for calendars."

She stared straight ahead, thinking of their next step. Then she looked at Bob again. "You're an angel."

"Yes. I haven't been fired yet."

"You can get fired from being an angel?"

He averted his eyes.

She gave him ample time to answer.

He didn't.

"Can't you find out where she lives?"

"And how would you like me to do that?"

"I don't know. Use your angel juice. Isn't it on her driver's license?"

He didn't answer, but his posture stiffened.

"Can't you use your X-ray vision to look at her driver's license?"

"I don't think I should do that," he said after a pause.

"What about her vehicle registration? It's in her glove box, I'm sure."

There was a longer hesitation this time. "I still don't think I should ..."

"Well, can you ask the daycare angel?" She was growing impatient.

Bob scowled. "No! Stop! What you're planning is illegal and unethical. I can't use God's power to do these things."

"What?" she cried. "Since when? What's the difference between peeking at her license and opening locked doors?"

Bob looked down sheepishly.

"Oh no, have you gotten in trouble, Bob?"

He didn't answer her.

"Fine. I'll do it myself." She put the car in reverse and backed out of Ethel's driveway.

"How?"

"I don't know yet." She drove toward downtown.

Bob was quiet for a few minutes, and she kept looking to make sure he was still there. "Does her social media profile give a town at least?"

"No. It's locked up tight as a drum. But I assume she lives in Plainfield."

"Why do you assume that?"

"Because she works in Plainfield and she dances in Plainfield."

"But what if she lives in Weld? She's certainly not going to work or dance there. The closest working and dancing would be in Plainfield, and that would go for any other town within fifty miles."

He had a point.

"Fine. Maybe she lives in Weld." Sandra hoped not. She didn't want to drive that far into the boonies again. Not after she'd had so much fun on their little expedition to Phillips.

She slowed when she neared All My Children Daycare.

"Are you sure this is even the right daycare?"

"Yes. Joyelle didn't withhold *everything*." For stealth's sake, she drove past the daycare.

Bob raised an eyebrow, but he didn't comment.

She parked in front of the bank. Then she put on her reffing cap and pulled it down over her eyes.

Bob rolled his eyes.

She added some sunglasses and then looked in the rearview mirror. Yup, pretty nondescript. She rested her hand on the door handle. "Are you going to wait here?"

"No. I'm going to come watch, but I have nothing to do with this. I do not support this, nor will I swoop to your rescue if you get caught."

Sandra hesitated. Did this mission go against Nate's rules then? Nate had said she couldn't investigate without Bob. "You'd let her kill me?"

He rolled his eyes again. "That's preposterous! She's not going to try to kill you in broad daylight in the middle of town in a daycare parking lot!"

"But if she tried to, you'd let her?"

He narrowed his eyes. "You'd better hurry up."

"Fine." She got out of the van. Keeping her head down, she approached the large brick building full of infants and toddlers. She met someone who gave her a chipper "Good morning!" but she ignored her and then felt guilty for doing so. If being a sleuth made her rude, then maybe she shouldn't be a sleuth anymore.

This was a good thought, one she would attend to as soon as she finished this case. She glanced around to make sure no one was watching her, and when it appeared that no one was, she turned ninety degrees to her left. Wondering how many security cameras were pointed her way, she followed the side of the building to the back parking lot, which was tiny. The backyard was a fenced-in mulched area with a small playground. Alongside the fence, three cars were parked.

On Tuesday nights, nearly every car in Joyelle's parking lot sported a Synergy Dance decal on their back window. She hoped April's car was one of those. If not, she was going to have to guess. As she got closer, she sighed with relief.

A blue four-wheel-drive Ford pickup with a white dancer on the back. Beneath the dancer, *April*.

She bent her knees and slouched a bit, hoping to be closer to invisible. Then she wondered if moving like a drunk with bad knees would call *more* attention to herself, and she popped up straight as an arrow. She pulled her sleeve down over her fingers, gave the area another quick scan, and tried to open April's passenger side door.

It was locked.

Of course. No one locked their cars in Plainfield, Maine. Except for April. This made Sandra even more suspicious of her. She cupped her hands together and looked into the car to see what she could see. Maybe she had written a check and left it face-up on her dashboard so someone could come along and glean her home address.

No such luck. The car was spotless.

She heard someone cough and stood up straight to find a little boy on the other side of the chain-link fence. His tiny fingers clutched the fence, and his wide eyes stared right at her. She smiled at him, but the fear did not leave his face. She looked around, wondering why there was a solitary child wandering around in the backyard. Her instinct was to investigate, make sure that the providers knew where he was, but then how would she explain what she was doing on the scene?

So, against every fiber of her being, she slunk away, telling herself that he would be okay. He was fenced in. They'd find him eventually.

Embarrassed and frustrated at the failure of her mission, she returned to her minivan.

"How did that go?" Bob's smirk suggested he knew exactly how it went.

"Were you watching?"

"I was."

"Did you lock her car?" she cried.

"What? Why would I do that?"

"To foil my plan!"

"No, I did nothing to interfere with your mission."

Sandra started the car and then pulled off her hat and sunglasses. "Did you see the little boy?"

"Of course. And it's already taken care of."

She looked at him quickly. "What does that mean?"

"He had shut the door behind him. I opened it again so the adults would notice. He's already back inside."

Relief washed over her. "Thank you so much." She put the car in drive and turned on her signal.

"I didn't do it for you."

"I know, but I still thank you."

Chapter 40

"Now what?" Bob asked.

"I have no idea." Traffic was thick, and Sandra was still trying to pull her van out into it, but no one was letting her.

"We could wait till April gets out of work and then follow her home."

"What good would that do? Then she'd be home. Pretty hard to snoop around her house with her in it."

"Right. We'd have to wait till tomorrow."

"I don't want to wait till tomorrow." Sandra flinched at how petulant she sounded. "Besides, I have a game today. And don't you as well?"

"Oh yeah, that's right."

Hopelessness was creeping in. Maybe she couldn't solve this one. Maybe she should just give up. A new idea occurred to her. "What if we broke into Synergy?"

"What? Why?"

"Joyelle must have records, right? She must have April's home address written down somewhere."

"I have no idea if that's true, but that is a *very bad* idea." He jerked as if he'd been stung, and then he disappeared.

What was that? Was he all right? Nonsensically, she turned and looked into the back of her van as if he might only have been bumped back a seat. Of course, the van was empty. She turned her blinker off, turned her van off, and chewed on her thumbnail.

She was worried about Bob, and she didn't know what to do. There was nothing *to* do. She might as well go relieve Ethel of her babysitting duty. With a long sigh, she started the van again, and immediately, Bob popped back into it.

"Where did you go?" she cried.

"I have an address."

"What? You said you wouldn't get it for me."

"I *didn't* get it for you. The dance angel got it for you. April has a post office box in Phillips, but she actually lives on an unnamed road in Township Six North of Weld."

"North of Weld?" Sandra screeched. This case was going to kill her.

"Yes, the location is north of Weld, but that's also the name of the township."

"What?"

"The name of the township is *Township Six North of Weld*."

"Huh. Isn't that catchy."

"Indeed. Do you know how to get there?"

"Of course not." She opened her maps app, but it couldn't find any results for a location of that name.

"Head toward Phillips. We'll figure it out."

She didn't want to go back to Phillips. But she did. Then she headed west, figuring that if Weld was southwest of Phillips, then the goofy township was probably west of Phillips.

Her plan failed. They ended up in Madrid, and all signs pointed to Rangeley.

"I don't think we should go to Rangeley," Bob said.

"I'm not doing it on purpose! There's only one road."

"Yes. Turn around, and then we'll take the first road that we see on the right."

They had passed a few dirt roads on their way to Madrid. "Those weren't roads."

"I know. It's either that or we go on foot."

Sandra slowed as she approached the first dirt turn off, and coming this way, they could see a small, ancient wooden sign that read "Number 6 Road."

"That's promising!" She turned her van onto the mysterious trail with more confidence. The road was wider, smoother, and more traveled than she'd first imagined. Her burgeoning sleuthing career had taken her on scarier roads than this. And only a mile down the road, they came to a small, well-kept trailer on the right. "That must be it."

"It may very well not be."

She drove past the driveway, looking for another place to pull off.

Bob snorted. "Are you worried about all the passing traffic seeing your car?"

"Yes." She found an old skidder trail with grass growing in the middle and pulled her van onto it. She drove a ways down it and then parked. "Let's go for a walk."

"I'll meet you there."

The crisp autumn air made for few mosquitoes, and Sandra was grateful. Though she parked in the woods, she opted to travel the road, promising herself that if she heard any cars coming, she would dive back into the tickletuppy.

But no one came, and she walked across what she believed to be April's yard without witness.

The front door was locked. This increased her confidence in two areas: first, that this was April's home; and second, that she was the killer. Why would someone lock their door way out here in the boonies unless they had something to hide? "Can you open it for me?" she asked into the stillness.

"No."

If she could have seen him, she would have shaken a fist at him. She circled the trailer, looking for an open window. "Come on, Bob. How else am I supposed to get in?"

He didn't answer.

"The dance angel wants this case solved. He gave you this address. He *wants* you to go inside."

Still no answer, but she heard a click at the front of the trailer, and she hurried around to try the door again. This time, it opened easily, and she found Bob standing inside. "I still think this is wrong."

"Then don't do anything. Just stand watch." She stepped into the dim light of the spotless living room. The blue curtains were drawn, and the whole room had a blue tint that, while it was pretty, made it difficult to see. She turned on her phone's flashlight and gasped. Several deer racks were mounted on the opposing wall. On the adjacent wall hung a stretched-out bearskin. Oh, April was *so* the killer.

Sandra went to the bookcase. It had worked before.

But this time, there were no books about the history of Mount Green, Michigan. There were no books at all really. There was a dictionary, an old Bible, and some photo albums. She pulled one of the albums out and flipped it open to find a page of cute baby photos. She turned the page, and the baby was blowing out a single candle on a cake. On the next page, the baby wasn't a baby anymore. She was a three or four-year-old on a stage wearing a tutu and cat ears. Sandra kept turning the pages, watching April grow up as she did so: April on horseback, at birthday parties, swimming with friends, kissing an old man on the cheek, kneeling beside a dead deer with a rifle across her knee, then again on stage, but older now ...

Then in a cap and gown in front of a school. Sandra peered at the picture, trying to see a school name, but she couldn't find one. She opened a browser on her phone, intending to look for a picture of Mount Green High School and see if they matched, but she had no signal. Stupid Township Six North of Weld. And unlike the generous Ivan Clark, April was unwilling to share her Wi-Fi. Sandra flipped the page, but the rest of the book was empty.

"Learn anything?"

"Not yet." She returned the album to its spot and pulled out the next one, but this album was dedicated solely to dogs. Puppies and then grown dogs. Adorable, but not helpful. She was just about to flip the book shut when something caught her eye. A close-up of a gorgeous chocolate lab, wearing a tag, and on that tag, "Bella Rose, 13 Grove St., Mount Green, MI." She gasped.

Bob leaned in for a closer look and then whistled. "It's no smoking gun, but I'm no longer saying you're wrong about her."

"I'm right."

The sound of an approaching engine froze them both for a second, but then they leapt up and hurried for the front door.

"It's too late!" Bob said. "She's here. Hide!"

Hide? Sandra looked around. Hide where? She ran down the hallway looking for a spot.

The trailer was small and infuriatingly neat. There were no hiding spots. She hurried into the dark bedroom, shining her light around the room. These curtains were drawn too, but they were black, and hardly any light was getting through. She slid the closet door open and jumped inside just as she heard the front door of the trailer open. Then she very slowly slid the closet door shut behind her, wondering where Bob had ended up.

She looked down at her phone to turn off the flashlight, and that's when she saw the plastic gun case leaning against the wall beside her.

Chapter 41

Sandra held her breath, afraid that the killer would hear her breathing in the quiet trailer in the middle of the forest. She stared into the darkness, looking toward the gun case without seeing it. Should she open the case and come out guns a'blazing? What were the chances that April had more than one gun?

She had no idea.

Nor did she think she could unsnap a gun case without being heard. And then what? What if the gun wasn't loaded? Where were the bullets? And even if she had the bullets, would she be able to figure out how to load them? She vowed to pay closer attention to how the cops on television used their guns. Not that this would help much now. She couldn't think of a single TV cop who carried around a giant rifle.

She needed a plan. And crouching in the closet waiting for the killer to reach in and grab her gun was a bad plan. She should at least have a hold of it, even if she didn't use it. Yes, that was it. Not a good plan, but better than just standing there. She would take the gun out of its case and hold it and try not to shoot anyone, herself included. If April came for her, she could at least swing it like a club.

Noise from the kitchen gave her an opportunity to flip open the tabs on the gun case. The clicks were deafening. She stopped moving and waited to hear April coming for her, but there was only the same rustling from the kitchen. *Bob, where are you?* She forced herself to breathe and then opened the gun case. She gingerly felt around in the darkness until her hand rested on the cold barrel of the weapon. She lightly slid her hand down until she found a way to easily pick up the gun. Then she pulled it toward her. Something brushed against her arm, and, assuming it was the worst of creepy-crawly beings, she almost shrieked, but then she realized it was only a strap attached to the gun. She held the gun to her and prayed Bob was about to do something clever so that April would never see just how clueless she was with this thing.

Footsteps came down the hall, and then a light clicked on the bedroom. Sandra pulled her feet back from the door, though this was silly. April—she assumed the person in April's bedroom was April—couldn't see under the door. Sandra strained to listen. The unseen person set something down, probably on the nightstand. Then the squeak of bed springs. The click of the remote. And then the television. Sandra's breath rushed out of her. She should be able to breathe now, as long as her breath wasn't louder than the TV.

April flipped through the channels and then stopped. For a moment there was no sound. Then there was a chime as if she'd started an app. A few more seconds of silence and then the distinctive *dung-dung* that could only mean one thing: *Law & Order.* The murderer was going to watch some cops catch a murderer. Sandra closed her eyes. How long was April going to stay in bed? One episode? Two? She didn't know if she could survive a marathon. And why was April home in the middle of the day, watching television?

"What are you planning on doing with *that*?" Bob asked, sounding horrified. Then he quickly added, "Don't answer me."

She hadn't planned on it.

"She's watching television," he said in her head.

I know, she thought, wishing she could speak into his head.

"She's crying."

Oh. That stopped her for a second. Crying about what? Was she feeling remorseful? Or was she only scared of getting caught? And why was Bob just standing there watching her cry? Couldn't he create some diversion to get his partner out of this closet?

"Oh, I like this episode," Bob said, and Sandra wanted to strangle him. "It's the one about the Russian mob."

Sandra had only watched a few reruns of the show and still knew that this description described multiple episodes.

Bob fell quiet, and Sandra listened to the show. Surprisingly, there was some comfort in having something to focus on, and she was able to follow the story without seeing the visuals.

She was paying such close attention that she didn't hear the new sound at first. It crept up on her, and it wasn't until a pause in the show's action that she noticed it.

Snoring.

April was asleep.

Or was she? Maybe she had realized someone was in her closet and was pretending to be asleep so that they would show themselves and let her shoot them. She waited for Bob to advise her, but he didn't. Had he left her there in the closet? Panic threatened to take her, but she fought back. She had to get out of this closet. She slid the door open a hair, flinching at the creak it made. But the snoring continued steadily. She slid the door open a few inches, and now she could peek out.

April lay on her side, facing away from Sandra. Thank goodness. Sandra opened the door some more and then slid out. She paused and slid the door back into place. She didn't like risking the sound, but she was taking the gun with her, and the longer it was before April knew that, the better.

A glass of water and an open pill bottle sat on the nightstand beside April's bed. Sandra was sure that hadn't been there before. What was going on? She'd come home in the middle of the day so upset that she had to take some medicine and go to sleep? Sandra was itching to creep closer and see what the medication was, but she didn't want to chance getting that close to the sleeping suspect.

So, holding the gun out in front of her with both hands, she backed out of the bedroom, keeping her eyes on the beautiful killer's back. Once she was in the hallway, she turned and scurried toward the front door. Then she was outside and running across the yard, holding the gun out in front of her with both hands, breathing hard just because she could, and then she was safe inside her minivan. She started the van and backed out onto the road. Then she stopped. Which way? Would April hear her drive by her house and get suspicious? She looked the other way. Did the road even *go* anywhere if she turned right? She didn't want to chance it. She turned left and crept back by April's house, hoping she was still asleep.

She didn't have a lot of time before she had to head to her soccer game. Once she was back on the tar, she sped toward Plainfield. At a red light, she called Chip and put him on speakerphone.

"I found the murder weapon."

"You what?"

"I have the gun. Can you meet me at my house?"

"Yes, when?"

"I'll be there in thirty."

Chapter 42

"That's not the murder weapon," Chip said when she pulled it out of her van.

"What do you mean?"

"Where did you get that?" Slaughter asked.

Sandra almost asked Chip why he'd brought her. "I got it at April's house. I told you, she did it."

"Not with that gun she didn't."

"What do you mean?" she asked again.

Slaughter closed her eyes as if Sandra exhausted her. "We know the caliber of the weapon used to kill Mr. Clark, and that's not it."

Sandra looked down at the gun in her hands. "This isn't a two-forty-three?"

Slaughter started. "How did you know he was killed with a two-forty-three?"

"Um … I didn't. But I thought … I thought this was a two-forty-three."

Slaughter narrowed her eyes. "You're not making any sense."

"Never mind that," Chip said, for once sounding more annoyed than Slaughter. "You were in her house? When?"

"Right before I called you."

"And did you break in?"

"I did not."

"So, she invited you in?"

"Not exactly."

They waited for her to say more. "The door was open."

"The door was open," Chip said slowly. "Doors around you are always mysteriously left open." He sighed. "So you decided to go through this *open door* and steal her shotgun?"

Sandra held the gun out to him. She suddenly couldn't stand to hold it. "I didn't *steal* it. I brought it to you. I'm sorry. I really thought it was the murder weapon."

"Why did you think that?" Slaughter asked.

Chip took the gun.

"Because it was in her closet, and she's a murderer. I didn't know she had a gun collection."

"Did anyone see you?" Chip's anger was mixed with concern.

"No."

"Sandra, you usually have a knack for figuring these crimes out, I'll give you that."

Slaughter rolled her eyes.

"But I'm going to ask you to sit this one out. You seem to be missing the mark here."

"I'm not missing anything. She's from Mount Green, Michigan. Jazmyn was from Mount

Green, Michigan. Jazmyn killed a woman there, and I think April followed her here to get revenge."

They both stopped. Had they seriously not thought of such a scenario?

"And Ivan Clark?" Slaughter said with a tone that says "Check" in a chess match.

"Ivan figured it out. He knew April did it, so she took care of him too. I heard her crying. Please, bring her in for questioning. I think she'll crumble."

Chip seemed to be considering it. "All right."

"All right?" Slaughter cried.

Sandra smiled. "Thank you. Sorry I took the wrong gun. But she's still the killer."

Chip nodded. "We'll bring her in on one condition."

"Name it."

"You sit the rest of this one out."

"Deal." She said it without thinking.

They left without another word, and Sandra turned to go into the house. She had to call Ethel and ask her to continue her childcare services through a soccer game, but first, she was *starving.* She was watching her feet, so she didn't notice Bob standing at the top of her steps until she almost ran into him. "Where did you go?" She went around him to get to her door, knowing how that would look to anyone who might be watching.

He turned and followed her inside. "Sorry, I had another crisis."

"A crisis more pressing than me being trapped in a closet in a murderer's trailer?"

"Yes, more pressing. I am an angel, remember? I have a lot of responsibilities."

You are a middle school soccer angel, Sandra thought but kept it to herself. "Fine." She ripped open the fridge. "You missed it. I made a fool out of myself."

"What?"

"It was the wrong size gun." She pulled out sandwich fixings, annoyed to see that someone had left behind a single slice of turkey. This was going to be a thin sandwich. "But the good news is Chip listened to me about Mount Green, and he's going to bring April in for questioning."

"Good. I noticed a framed picture of a woman on her dresser. Looked like her. I think it was her mother."

"It probably was." She slathered on the mayo to try to make up for the paltry turkey supply.

"The frame said, 'Gone but not forgotten.'"

245

"Oh." This struck a chord. She put the mayo down and looked at the angel. "Now that you mention it, I saw April on a video dedicating a dance trophy to her mother, and she did seem sad for someone winning a trophy. That would make sense, though, if she'd lost her mom." Sandra's throat tightened. April was a killer, but if she'd lost her mom when she was young? How painful that must have been. "Wait, don't we know the victim's name?"

"Yes, we do. Shawna Pevzner."

"Maybe that's April's last name?"

"No idea. Hang on." He vanished.

Sandra shook her head and turned back to her sandwich. Maybe it would make more sense to bring the dance angel into their circle instead of popping out every few minutes to ask him a question.

Bob reappeared. "Her name is April Wilson."

"So *not* the daughter of Shawna Pevzner."

"Could still be. Wilson could be her father's name. Or a married name. Or she could have changed her name, as Jazmyn did."

"True." She licked some renegade mayonnaise off her finger and dropped the knife into the sink. "I bet you're right. But I promised I wouldn't do anything more. So,

246

let's let Chip do his thing and see what he finds out."

"Will he tell you what he finds out?"

"Yes, he will." She winked at her angel. "One way or the other."

Chapter 43

The hours and then the days ticked by with no word from Chip. Come Tuesday, Sandra couldn't stand it anymore. She texted him. "Did you question her?"

"Not yet."

She wanted to scream. "Why not?" She resisted the urge to use all caps.

"Haven't been able to locate her."

"What?"

"She packed a bag and hasn't been back to work. My guess is someone broke into her home and spooked her."

Oops. Sandra didn't know how to respond to that. "Sorry." She hit send and then had another thought. "Did you find another gun?"

"We don't have a search warrant."

"Want me to go have another look?"

"NO!" All caps.

She considered doing it anyway. She looked at the clock. She had a meeting at church, and then she had to pick the kids up from school, then run Peter and Joanna to their soccer practices, then pick them up, and then get Joanna to dance. Somewhere in there, she should probably get some dinner on the table. Did she have time to run to

Township Six North of Weld? Probably not. She vowed to go in the morning.

"She might come to dance class tonight. I think dance is important to her."

"We'll be there."

Sandra got out of the van at Synergy and looked around the parking lot, expecting to see a stakeout vehicle.

She saw nothing of the sort.

Disappointed, she took Joanna's hand and let herself be led into the building. The lobby was full of girls zipping around to and fro, yet Joyelle broke through the storm to reach Sandra. "What happened to April?" she asked, her voice laden with accusation.

"I have no idea."

Joanna broke off to go inspect the snack table.

"The police questioned me! Apparently she's missing?"

Sandra wasn't sure missing was the right word. "They told me she packed a bag. I'm assuming she took a trip?" Kind of a lame statement, but she was trying not to offend Joyelle.

"Took a trip?!" Joyelle was offended.

One of Joanna's classmates threw her arms around Joyelle, who bent to embrace the girl. "Hi, honey. How was your week?" Joyelle gave the child her undivided attention, but as soon as the update was over, Joyelle's face grew serious as her eyes flicked back to Sandra's. "Took a trip where?"

Sandra looked around. Some of the moms were staring at them. "Could we go in the studio for a second?"

Joyelle nodded and led the way. Once they were out of the crowd, Sandra asked Joyelle if she knew about the death of Shawna Pevzner. She did not. Sandra filled her in. Joyelle gasped, and her eyes filled with tears. She stopped defending April.

"I'm not saying April is evil. But I do think she killed Jazmyn."

"Donna," Joyelle said tonelessly.

"Yes. I think she killed Donna Smith because Donna Smith killed her mother."

Joyelle nodded and turned toward the front of the room. Sandra stepped out of the studio and back into the fray of the lobby.

"Is Miss Joyelle okay, Mama?"

"Yes. She's just sad because people have died."

Joanna nodded thoughtfully. "It's always sad when people die."

"Yes, honey. It is." She kissed her daughter on the forehead and then bent to help her tie the thick ribbons of her tap shoes. She straightened up and watched her daughter bounce into the studio, feeling a good dose of pride at the sight.

She tried to get comfortable and settled in to play some more Egg Wars, but she kept getting killed because she was thinking about April, not the tasks of the game. Had April simply gone back to Michigan? Was there anything to go back to there? If April fled the state, she might never be found, and even if she was, Sandra wouldn't be the one to find her. This thought made Sandra sad.

As Joanna's class time drew near its end, Sandra eyed the door nervously. It would be insane for April to show up for dance class, and yet, Sandra hoped she would. She heard the roar of an approaching motorcycle, and then Jess breezed through the door. Astrid followed close behind. Then came the pregnant woman—Sandra still didn't know her name, but goodness was she pregnant! The door stayed shut for several minutes and then

Mandi arrived. Then came Tiffany with her Bluetooth. But no April.

The young girls came out excitedly chatting about their class. Sandra half-listened to Joanna's account and then, after giving her a hug and surrendering her cell phone to her, got up to go into class. It was past time. Then the door opened again, and in came Gertrude.

Sandra wandered over to the door and looked out for the stakeout, and there they were, as obvious as daylight: Chip and Slaughter in a suspiciously clean black SUV. If April had planned on dance class, she would change her mind at the sight of that.

Chapter 44

Sandra was the last student to leave the studio. For Joyelle's sake, she had waited for Gertrude to leave and then had followed her out—to make sure she really left.

Sandra smiled and nodded to Calvin and then followed Joanna to their minivan. Out of the corner of her eye, she saw Calvin drive away. The stakeout vehicle was gone, but she had the strangest sense that she was being watched.

"Mama, the seatbelt is stuck again."

The seatbelt was stuck more often than it was unstuck. It was an old minivan. "Hang on, I'll come get it." As she wrestled with the deteriorating safety device, part of her was aware that Joyelle came out of the building, got into her car, and drove away.

"Hurry!" Bob cried from out of nowhere. And then he was in the front passenger seat.

"Hurry what?" She continued to yank at Joanna's seatbelt.

"Can't she sit in a different seat?"

"This is my seat!"

"Just give me a second." She pulled harder.

Suddenly, Bob was beside her, and the seatbelt came free.

Joanna giggled. "Nice job, Bob!"

Sandra slid the door shut, and Bob was back in the front. "Let's go!"

Sandra jumped into the front. "What are you so wound up about?"

"April is following Gertrude."

"How do you know that?"

"I saw her with my eyeballs. She was parked across the street. Go, go, go!"

"Bob, I'm not getting into a high-speed chase with my child in the car."

"Since when?"

"Since I lost sleep for weeks after doing it last time! And that was different!" She wasn't sure how that time was different, but she was desperate to defend herself.

"Please drive!" Bob pressed on the dashboard as if that would make the van move.

"We've already lost them."

"We can find them."

"No." The more Sandra argued, the more resolute she became.

"Gertrude could be in danger!"

Her resolution wavered. "Let's call Chip then." She reached for her phone, but there was nothing there. "Joanna? Where's my phone?"

"Oh no."

"Joanna?"

"Please drive!"

"Where's my phone, Joanna? And why do you need me to drive? Can't you fly?"

"I don't need you to drive. I need you to interfere when we get there. Once you get going, I'll go ahead and tell you where they've gone. But I dare not go ahead as I don't really trust you to get going!"

"I'll call Chip. Let me go back in—" She remembered that Joyelle had already left. "All right. Go ahead. Tell me where to go. But if I think for even one second that Joanna is in danger, I'm out."

"Go, Mama, go!"

Sandra started the car, and Bob disappeared. Again.

She stopped at the end of the drive. "Which way, Bob?" she called out to no one.

No one answered.

After thirty seconds of waiting, Joanna said, "Just guess, Mama!"

Sandra hesitated. She didn't want to be wrong. But she also didn't want to continue sitting on the side of the road, a spectacle. She turned left and drove. Every few minutes, she called out to Bob to see if he was within earshot, but no one answered.

"Where are we going?" Joanna asked, sounding as though she were having too much fun.

"You're the one who told me to guess. I have no idea where we're going, honey."

Joanna giggled, and Sandra continued south on 27. Then she had a thought. Gertrude had said she lived in Somerset County. This wasn't a great clue because Somerset County was monstrous, but right now, they weren't headed toward it. She pulled into the parking lot of a convenience store claiming to offer the original brownie whoopie pie. Her stomach rumbled, and her mouth watered, but she ignored the craving in the name of saving Gertrude. Maybe. Maybe Gertrude wouldn't need to be saved, and she could come back for a brownie whoopie pie.

She opened her glovebox and rooted around, unsure she even owned a paper map anymore. Eureka! Score one for never cleaning out the glovebox. She unfolded the old map and took a look. Oh good, she wasn't so far from Somerset County after all. She just needed to stay on Route 2. She pulled out of the parking lot and turned left, heading east, away from whoopie pie temptation.

Bob reappeared.

"What took you so long?"

"I got distracted."

"By Gertrude?"

"No, by a football injury in Skowhegan."

"You've got to be kidding."

He leveled a sober gaze at her. "I never kid about football."

"Did you see if April is really following Gertrude?"

"I'm positive. Gertrude stopped for some pizza and a slushie, and April waited across the street with her headlights off." Bob shuddered.

"A slushie? What is she, five?"

Bob shook his head. "She is not five. But she did put five different flavors into one cup."

Joanna giggled. "I like Gertrude."

"Lots of people seem to," Bob said. "Anyway, I'm going back to watch, but her little pit stop bought you some time."

"Wait!" Sandra cried. "I don't even know where I'm going!"

Bob told her the address. Interesting. She hadn't been through Mattawooptock in years. She never had a reason to go there. She thought this was the case with most people.

Chapter 45

Gertrude lived in a trailer park. Sandra turned in but then slowed to a crawl. She wasn't sure how to proceed. She didn't know what she was driving into, and she didn't want to put Joanna in harm's way.

"Mama, we're not moving."

It was true. She had stopped in the narrow road. She tapped her thumb on the steering wheel, trying to make up her mind. She hated being indecisive.

Bob reappeared. "We've got to hurry. Don't worry about Joanna. Macholyadah is here."

It took a second to remember who that was. Then she was astounded. "He is?" She looked around in the dark. "Where?"

"Right beside Joanna."

Joanna gasped.

Sandra looked in the rearview mirror but couldn't see her daughter's face in the darkness.

"Keep driving," Bob said.

Sandra gingerly stepped on the gas.

"Gertrude is in trailer number three. April is trying to break in through the back—"

"What?" She stomped on the brake. "We should call the police!"

"Fine. You do that with the cell phone you left locked in a dance studio."

Sandra growled. If she was going to keep this up, she would need to get a key from Joyelle. She tapped the gas pedal again, and the van rolled forward. Seconds later, they were parked in front of trailer number three. "What do I do?" Sandra whispered.

"Let's go in." He was no longer in the van.

"Wait!" She tried to whisper loudly, and it sounded like a hiss. She rolled down his window and leaned over. "Do you promise that Macho …" That wasn't quite right. She tried again, "Mawcko …" She couldn't do it. "Do you swear that the dance angel is here?"

Bob frowned. "I would not tell a lie. He's right beside her. Now, come on!"

Sandra studied him. Was he telling the truth? He had to be, right? She wished she had Gertrude's ability to sniff out fibs.

Bob was headed up Gertrude's front steps.

Fine. She unbuckled and climbed out of the van. Then she turned to look at her daughter. "Be right back, honey. If you need anything, ask the angel." She looked at the empty seat beside Joanna. Joanna looked too, and her face lit up in a wide smile. "Can you see him?"

Sandra asked softly, suddenly feeling reverent.

Joanna looked at her. "Can't you?"

"Come on!" Bob hollered, his hand on the doorknob.

Sandra slammed the van door and ran to Bob, who was now knocking.

"Holler to her. Tell her to let us in," Bob commanded.

"Gertrude!" Sandra shouted.

No one answered.

"Gertrude!" she shouted again more loudly.

"I'll do it." The door sprang open a few inches.

"Hey there!" a voice shouted from behind. The voice was obviously from an older person, but the authority in it made a chill dance up her spine, as if she'd been caught red-handed at something particularly wretched.

She spun around to look.

It was Calvin. "You!" he cried. "What are you doing?"

"Gertrude's in trouble!" She ducked into the dark trailer and was immediately disoriented. What little light filtered in through the curtains lit what looked like mountains of boxes. Was this Gertrude's home? Or some weird trailer warehouse? She looked around for Bob but couldn't see him. "Gertrude?" she called.

A crash sounded from deeper in the trailer, and a woman whimpered. The whimper sounded too dainty to be Gertrude.

"April, stop," Sandra said, trying to use her firm ref voice.

April didn't stop. Sandra heard her moving about, and then she smashed into something else.

"Gertrude! Where are you?" Sandra tried to head toward the sounds, but she couldn't find an opening in the mountain of boxes. Had April built a barricade? That didn't make sense.

She heard Calvin step in behind her.

Something above Sandra wailed, and her heart nearly stopped as the being flew over her head so close she could feel it. She whirled around to look into the darkness, and the light from the window reflected in the thing's eyes, making them glow green. Good grief, it was only a cat. She turned back around to find herself staring directly into the face of another. "Excuse me, kitty." She started to move the boxes, thinking she'd have to dig her way through the room, but then the first cat—the scary one—walked directly through the stacks.

Sandra saw her tail vanish into the boxes and moved in that direction, running her hand along the boxes as she went. Her eyes were starting to adjust, but she still had a feeling the place was booby-trapped.

Sure enough, there was the opening. Calvin flicked on the lights, momentarily blinding her. Why hadn't he done that sooner? He probably hadn't been able to find a light switch.

Now she could clearly see the maze in front of her. Indeed, Gertrude's living room was full of boxes and totes stacked neatly from floor to ceiling. It reminded her of the prop room at her son's theater, except nothing was labeled. She weaved through the stacks, counting one, two, three, four cats watching her as she went. The original cat who had led her into this tunnel had disappeared.

Sandra could see that the path opened out ahead of her, and she sped up to get to that open space, feeling a bit claustrophobic. But before she could reach the clearing, the wall beside her wobbled and then was falling directly at her. She tried to put an arm out, but she was too late. An incredibly heavy box hit her in the head, and she saw stars.

Chapter 46

The falling tower of boxes had knocked Sandra sprawling into the clearing. She sat up rubbing her head. She heard moaning. The avalanche had taken out Calvin. She scrambled over to dig him out.

Sandra saw a flash of movement in her peripheral vision—it was pink, so this one wasn't a cat—but she ignored it to help Calvin.

"You get him! I'll go get Gertrude!" Bob said.

Couldn't Bob have protected her from this particular injury? Her head was ringing. She hurried to pull the boxes off the pile they'd landed in, and some of them shifted beneath her hands as Calvin tried to wiggle his way out. She went as fast as she could, and then his head appeared. "Are you all right?"

"I'm fine, I'm fine!" His level of anger suggested he was in good health. He tried to sit up and got stuck.

"Hang on." She pulled another box toward her, but this one was heavy. She grunted as she yanked. "What is in this thing?"

"I think that's where Gertrude keeps her cast iron cat collection."

One of the boxes had opened, and a dozen pairs of sneakers had spilled out. Many of them still had tags on them.

Finally, Calvin was mostly free. She held out a hand to help him up, but he ignored it, so she turned and left him on the floor. She hurried down the hallway toward April's voice. She rushed past the bathroom toward the bedroom, but then realized she'd gone too far. The stacks of boxes lining the hallway made it easier to backpedal than to turn around, so she did, smashing directly into Calvin as he reached the bathroom from the other direction.

"Ow!" he cried.

April let out a primal howl of rage. "What is wrong with you people?!" she screamed, completely unhinged. "Why can't you mind your own business?"

Sandra stopped moving. She stood still, her hip pressed against Calvin's hip, staring into the tiny bathroom, which was made smaller by the many items in it. Gertrude stood in the middle of the room leaning on her walker. She wore a thick, fluorescent pink bathrobe and an orange towel on her head. Cats swirled around her feet. One cat was not swirling and was standing with her hair raised, hissing at April, who held a rifle pointed at Gertrude. Her well-manicured finger was on the trigger.

"Easy, Monsoon," Gertrude said to the protective cat.

Sandra hazarded a glance at April, whose eyes were wild with panic. Bob stood right beside her. He could easily grab the gun if he needed to. This sight was tremendously comforting, and Sandra exhaled before saying, "It's all right, Gertrude. Don't be scared."

"It's not all right!" Gertrude cawed. "This crazy dancing lady has a rifle!"

"I know." Sandra boldly stepped into the bathroom. "But she's not going to shoot us."

April gave her a dirty look.

"I am so sorry for your loss, April. I don't know, if I had been in your shoes, if I would have done any differently." She knew she wouldn't have changed her identity, moved across the country, and murdered two people, but she kept that to herself. "Lower your weapon, April. It's over. You know you can't kill all four of us before one of us gets you."

"Four?" Gertrude cried, her head swiveling. "Are you dumb, or should your math teacher be fired?"

Pretty sure her most recent math teacher had long-since retired, Sandra tried to be patient with the woman she was rescuing. "Three. I meant three."

April lowered her weapon a few inches. Now it was pointed at Gertrude's short legs.

Gertrude took this as an opportunity. She let out a wail and charged at April, walker and all.

Surprised, April staggered back into the wall. Her left hand let go of the rifle to try to push Gertrude off her, but Gertrude had her pinned. She started jabbing her fist into April's throat repeatedly. April made an awful choking sound and then brought the barrel of the rifle up against Gertrude's head.

"Aggh!" Gertrude cried, falling back.

Bob caught and righted her, but Gertrude was too stunned to notice his help.

Furious, Monsoon hissed loudly and leapt at April's face.

April screamed and brought her hand up to protect her face and staggered backward. The gun exploded, and the other cats bolted in a dozen different directions as Calvin lunged to grab the gun. Sandra looked around wildly to make sure no one had been hit. She checked the humans and then the cats but everyone appeared to be unscathed. She looked in the direction that the gun had been pointing and saw that April had blown a hole in a hanging hairdryer. Now that she was looking, she realized Gertrude had a dozen hairdryers hanging on the wall.

Calvin, looking like an experienced rifleman, pointed the gun at April, who was now crumpled against the wall, crying.

"Gert, call the police," Calvin said.

"I'm not calling Hale," Gertrude cried as if the idea were preposterous. She had her walker back under her and held one hand to her injured face. "He'll find a way to blame me for this!"

"Call Detective Chip Buker," Sandra said. "State Police."

Gertrude looked at her as if she were stupid. "I don't know that number. Do you? You're so good with numbers."

Sandra sighed. She really wished she hadn't forgotten her phone. "I don't have it memorized, but you can search for it—"

"Five-five-five …" Bob started.

Sandra glanced at him, and then repeated the number. "I just remembered. Five-five-five—"

Suddenly suspicious, Gertrude glanced over her shoulder and then back at Sandra. "Who are you talking to?"

"I'm not talking to anyone. I'm telling you Chip Buker's phone number."

Gertrude looked in Bob's direction again and then back at Sandra. "You're lying."

"Will you please call him?" Sandra snapped. She didn't know if April would remain so docile for long.

"I *can't* call him with you in my way." Gertrude pushed her way to the door. "I don't keep my cellular in the lavatory." She went through the doorway shaking her head. "Unsanitary," she mumbled as she left the room.

Sandra looked at Calvin, who was keeping his eyes on April.

"Why did you do it?" he asked.

"Wait for me!" Gertrude called.

Chapter 47

Gertrude reappeared in the doorway of her bathroom. She had removed the towel, and her orange hair stuck out in innumerable directions. It reminded Sandra of a torch lily in full bloom. "Why did you do it?" Gertrude demanded.

April had slid down the wall and was sitting on the floor with her head in her hands. One of Gertrude's more compassionate cats was rubbing up against her leg. The cat who had assaulted her and saved the day had disappeared. April whimpered.

"If you don't tell me, I will make this so much worse for you!" Gertrude said.

April looked up at her. "What?"

"I will tell them you tortured me! That you held my head underwater trying to get information out of me!"

"What information?"

"Doesn't matter!" Gertrude said matter-of-factly. "Who do you think they're going to believe, me or you?"

Sandra thought it might be a toss-up. She felt sorry for April even though she was a cold-blooded killer. "Donna killed April's mother a long time ago."

Gertrude gasped.

"She wanted revenge," Sandra explained.

"Is that the truth?" Gertrude asked.

Staring at the floor, April nodded.

Gertrude looked at Sandra approvingly. "You are better at this than I thought. You should be a gumshoe like me!" She turned back to April and then muttered, "But good luck getting licensed."

"Why did you kill Ivan?" Calvin asked, still holding the rifle steady.

Gertrude gave him a long look. "Let me do it," she said slowly. Then she looked at April. "Why did you kill Ivan?"

Sandra gave her a chance to answer, but she didn't. "I think Ivan figured it out. Is that right, April?"

April nodded.

"And she couldn't let him tell anyone who she really was."

"Oh mylanta! You are really good at this!" Gertrude appeared satisfied for a second, but then her eyes grew wide. "But why were you trying to shoot me? I hadn't figured anything out!" She pointed at Sandra. "You should have been trying to shoot her!"

April leaned her head back on the wall and exhaled slowly. "I wasn't going to shoot you. I was going to poison you, but I couldn't find my way to the kitchen."

Calvin snickered.

"Why couldn't you find your way to the kitchen?" Gertrude asked. "It's right beside the living room!"

Calvin coughed, obviously trying to stifle another laugh.

"Hey, how did you get in?" Gertrude asked April.

"Through a window."

Gertrude turned to Sandra. "And how did you get in?"

"Through the front door."

"You're lying," Gertrude said quickly.

"She's not lying," Calvin said. "I watched her walk right in."

"I had that door locked up tight! I don't leave doors unlocked when there are murderers out creeping around."

"I tried it," April said so quietly that Sandra almost didn't hear her. "It was locked."

Gertrude stuck her tongue out at Calvin. "See!" Then she glared at Sandra. "How did you get my door unlocked?"

Sandra ignored the question.

"I need better security," Gertrude mumbled. "But then again, maybe I don't as I'll be moving soon anyway."

They heard sirens.

"That was quick," Sandra said. Chip must have been in the vicinity.

"You still haven't said why you were trying to kill me," Gertrude said.

"I thought you'd figured it out. All those questions you were asking, and then you stole my gun—"

"Gun? What gun? I didn't steal your gun!"

April looked confused. "You didn't? Well, someone did. Someone broke into my house and stole my twelve-gauge."

Sandra tried to look innocent.

"It wasn't me," Gertrude said, glaring at Sandra.

April stared at the wall across from her. "Why do you have so many blow dryers?"

Gertrude looked at them. "Never know when you're going to need an extra."

Someone pounded on the front door.

"Someone should probably go help them navigate their way through the trailer," Calvin said.

Gertrude looked at Sandra expectantly.

"Fine." Sandra left the threesome behind. She met Chip halfway through the maze. "Gertrude is back here. Everyone's fine." She backed up until she could turn around, and then she led them the rest of the way to the bathroom. "Watch your step," she said as she went. "There are a lot of cats."

Chapter 48

Chip pulled April to her feet, handcuffed her, and read her her rights. Then he looked at Sandra. "Want to tell me what happened here?"

Sandra gave him a brief rundown.

Chip looked at Gertrude. "And you didn't hear someone banging around in your home?"

"I was taking a tubbie."

Chip raised an eyebrow. "A tubbie?"

"Yes." Gertrude looked around furtively and lowered her voice. "I call them tubbies. The word B-A-T-H," she spelled out, "scares the cats."

Obviously confused, Chip looked to Sandra for help. She didn't know what help she could give him.

Calvin, now holding the rifle casually at his side, as if he did so every day, stepped in. "She gives the cats baths, and she's gotten in the habit of calling them tubbies when she does so." For the first time, Sandra wondered if Gertrude was Monk and Calvin was her Natalie.

"I didn't realize that people bathed cats." Chip looked at Sandra again. "Thought they were a self-cleaning kind of thing."

"I get my besties from all over, and sometimes they need some help. When they're on the street, they don't have time for grooming, so I give them a head start on their cleaning. Then they can maintain it."

"I see," Chip said, though it was doubtful that he did. "So, you were in the tub. Still, it sounds as though your intruders made a lot of noise."

Why was he so suspicious of Gertrude?

"I don't know what to tell you," Gertrude said. "I was under the water. I can't hear anything when my ears are full of bubbles. I had just gotten out when this crazy lady came stomping into my private privy."

"I think private privy is redundant, Gert," Calvin said.

Gertrude gave a self-satisfied smile. "Thank you."

With a bewildered expression, Chip looked at Sandra. "All right. I'm going to take her in. Looks like you've done it again, Ms. Provost."

"Her?" Gertrude cried. "She didn't do anything!"

"She saved your life, Gertrude," Calvin said.

"Hardly! I had complete control of the situation!"

Chip gave April a little nudge. "Let's go." They headed toward the door, and Sandra followed.

"You didn't have complete control of anything," Calvin said. "You were in the bathtub!"

"I was *not* in the bathtub anymore, and *she* didn't save anything! I saved myself when I punched her in the throat! And then Monsoon extra-saved me when she jumped on the killer's face!"

"I wouldn't have been here to grab the gun if Sandra hadn't ..." Calvin's voice faded away.

Chip guided a weeping April through the stacks. "What *is* this place?" he muttered.

"I don't know. Gertrude sure does have a lot of stuff." They passed a pile of pizza boxes. Were those containers for something else? Or did she just save the pizza boxes? That was one mystery that Sandra was content not to solve.

She found Bob leaning against her minivan. He winked at her. "Nice work."

"Thanks. Couldn't have done it without you." She looked into her van. "Is Mawcko... is he still here?"

Bob smiled. "No, he's gone."

Sandra opened the door and stuck her head in. "Are you okay, honey?"

"I'm great! Macholyadah taught me how to do a pirouette!" His name rolled off her tongue as if she were fluent in Hebrew.

"In a minivan?" Sandra asked.

Joanna giggled. "No, silly. We danced in the street." She pointed out her window. "Right there."

Sandra looked at Bob, alarmed. "My daughter was dancing in the street with an angel? In the dark?" She looked around, wondering what onlookers might have thought of such a spectacle.

Bob placed a hand on her arm. "She was one hundred percent safe the entire time."

Joanna was oblivious to her mother's distress. "It was so fun, Mama! I can't wait to show Miss Joyelle!"

Her daughter's joy was contagious, so Sandra let go of the fear that was trying to destroy the moment. "Good, honey. I'm excited for that too. Miss Joyelle will be very proud of you. Probably shouldn't tell her that a dance angel taught you how, though."

"Oh, go ahead and tell her," Bob said. "But tell her not to tell anyone else."

Sandra was shocked. "Really?"

"Sure. Miss Joyelle can handle it. She's a dance teacher. They can handle just about anything."

Chapter 49

The thunder clapped so loudly that Sandra jumped. Moose and she had called their soccer game for weather, and now Sandra was driving home through the downpour. She could hardly see out of the windshield, and it didn't help that one of her windshield wipers was on its last leg.

She'd blocked all of her Tuesdays so she could get Joanna to and from dance, but her boss had begged her to take this one game. He didn't have anyone else, apparently, so she'd relented, and Nate had agreed to do dance duty.

She decided to stop at the studio, even though Nate was there. It was closer than home, and she wanted to get out of the rain.

She was a little nervous about seeing Joyelle again, but she tried to shake it off. Joyelle had seemed very understanding when Sandra had said she didn't think she would continue with dance class.

She pulled into Synergy's parking lot, parked, and got out into the downpour. It wasn't a big deal, as she was already soaked with sweat from running up and down the field in a hundred percent humidity. She looked up, and the sky was dark and angry. She hurried inside and then gasped at the air conditioning. It felt freezing cold to her wet skin, and she broke out in goosebumps.

Peter sat beside a window, looking down at a textbook. Sammy sat nearby, playing with a metal truck. Neither of her sons noticed her arrival.

Nate leaned on the sill of the viewing window. He was the only man in the room, and all the moms were seated. They were usually clustered around the window, and with amusement, Sandra wondered if her husband had scared them off. He glanced at her. "What are you doing here?"

She glanced outside.

He followed her gaze. "Oh yeah, I didn't think of that." He looked her up and down. "Have a nice bath?"

"Not a bath. A *tubbie*."

He frowned. "What?"

"Nothing." She leaned on the sill beside him, and he slid away.

"Ew, you're all wet."

She looked through the window. Joanna was with a group of girls seated on the floor, watching the other half of the class dance.

"She'll be going again soon," Nate said.

"I know."

"Have you talked to Bob?"

"Not since the arrest."

"So, he's not going to be your friend unless someone gets killed?"

Sandra chuckled. "That's not true. I'm sure he'd help out in any pinch I found myself in."

"You planning to find yourself in another one soon?" He was making light of the question, but she knew there was a gravity behind it.

"I won't ever investigate anything without checking with you. And no, I don't plan on seeking out crimes to solve." *Like Gertrude does,* she silently added. "But if one does fall into my path, I can't promise I will stay out of it."

"I suppose that makes sense. But I'd be thrilled if you did decide to hang up your magnifying glass."

"I'll keep that in mind."

Joanna's group took the floor and began to dance.

"She's amazing," Nate said, sounding reverent.

"I know."

"No, really." He flirtatiously bumped her elbow with his. "I get it now. Look at her. The way her face lights up when the music starts.

The way her movement lights up the whole room." He slid a hand around her wet waist. "You were right." He kissed her on the cheek. "This is really something." He turned his attention back to the window, and together they watched their daughter dance.

Joanna stepped forward lightly and began to spin, bringing her foot to her knee as she did so. She held her hands out delicately in front of her.

Her father gasped.

Joanna stopped the spin as gracefully as she'd begun it and extended her right arm out in front of her. Her face was beaming.

"That's our daughter?" Nate said.

"That's our daughter. And that was a pirouette. She was very excited to show that to Miss Joyelle today."

"I'll bet." He smiled at her again. "Okay, fine. I'll help you pay for the costumes."

She laughed. "It's okay. I get paid even when it rains."

"All right then. I'll pick her up sometimes." He said this as if he was doing her a big favor, but she suspected that he was also enjoying himself a little. They only had one dancer in the family, but she would have several fans.

MORE LARGE PRINT BOOKS
BY ROBIN MERRILL

Wing and a Prayer Mysteries
The Whistle Blower
The Showstopper
The Pinch Runner

Gertrude, Gumshoe Cozy Mystery Series
Introducing Gertrude, Gumshoe
Gertrude, Gumshoe: Murder at Goodwill
Gertrude, Gumshoe and the VardSale Villain
Gertrude, Gumshoe: Slam Is Murder
Gertrude, Gumshoe: Gunslinger City
Gertrude, Gumshoe and the Clearwater Curse

Shelter Trilogy
Shelter
Daniel
Revival

New Beginnings
Knocking
Kicking
Searching

The Prima Donna

Piercehaven Trilogy
Piercehaven
Windmills
Trespass

Robin also writes sweet romance
as Penelope Spark:

Sweet Country Music Romance
The Rising Star's Fake Girlfriend
The Diva's Bodyguard
The Songwriter's Rival

Clean Billionaire Romance
The Billionaire's Cure
The Billionaire's Secret Shoes
The Billionaire's Blizzard
The Billionaire's Chauffeuress
The Billionaire's Christmas

Want to stay in the loop? Visit robinmerrill.com
to join Robin's Readers and be the first to hear
about new releases.

Made in the USA
Las Vegas, NV
07 January 2021